THE MILLION DOLLAR
TYPEWRITER

Murray Segal

The Million Dollar Typewriter
Copyright 2017 by Murray Segal

Published by Piscataqua Press
142 Fleet St.
Portsmouth, NH 03801

www.ppressbooks.com

Printed in the United States of America

ISBN: 978-1-944393-46-5

FOR JANICE WAYNE

I have seen so many books dedicated to a wife or other loved one that it seems like a routine and almost meaningless thought. Trust me, this one has genuine meaning. There is no way in the world that this book would ever have seen the light of day without the help and encouragement of my wife, Janice Wayne. She endorsed the effort at the very beginning of the project and lifted me up many times when I was ready to quit. In addition to that help she was my I.T. department who managed to solve the dilemma of keeping the Toshiba going and dealing with the vagaries of Microsoft Word. She was the last one to read the book before it went off to the publisher. Thank you, Janice, from the very bottom of my heart. I love you dearly for all you have done for me over the years.

A TRIBUTE TO ENRICO FERMI

This story involves a typewriter that was in Fermi's research lab at Columbia University in New York. Fermi fled Italy with his Jewish wife just prior to the outbreak of WWII.

In order to raise the money necessary to continue his work on nuclear chain reactions, he wrote a letter to President Roosevelt and got Albert Einstein to sign it.

Roosevelt made the money available, and that led to the development of the atomic bomb. This beat Nazi Germany to the punch and ended the war. The free world owes Fermi a debt of gratitude. It is the author's opinion that he was the greatest hero to come out of that war.

The
Million Dollar
Typewriter

CHAPTER I – THE SETTING

.

I operate a typewriter business in Portsmouth, New Hampshire. Sure, typewriters are largely extinct but if you have one and need it repaired, I am the only shop. Not a bad situation. A series of strange events began here some time ago, but before I get into that let me enlighten you about this part of New Hampshire. Portsmouth is the center of this small region. It's only an hour's drive north of Boston and home to about 21,000 people. This is the same size it was in 1950. The Piscataqua River is the boundary with Maine to the north. It flows rapidly along the northern edge of the city and then empties into the Atlantic Ocean. Portsmouth grew up as a military place, from its beginning. The Portsmouth Naval Shipyard—which is really in nearby Kittery, Maine—is a major employer in the region. Over the years, the courts have heard arguments about whether the shipyard is in Maine or New Hampshire. They finally decided that it was north of the boundary line and thus in the state of

Maine. The shipyard dominated the place for a long time and still employs thousands of people who work on the Navy's nuclear submarines there. But Portsmouth is no longer a Navy Town. As far as I know there is not a single bordello left. The former Pease Airforce Base still houses a fleet of Air Force Tankers. Pease has the longest runway on the entire east coast at 12,000 feet.

Portsmouth is cuter than cute and is festooned with restaurants, boutiques and dozens of historical sites. It even has a substantial bookstore right downtown. Really. Which brings me back to the obsolete work that I do. I have a hobby which recently exploded into a real business thanks to an expertly maximized website created by my daughter, Lisa. This success later turned out to be a curse in disguise. More on my three children Karen, Lisa and Paul later.

CHAPTER II - A - ROUTINE DAY

My name is Murray Segal and I live with my child bride Janice in the town of Exeter, New Hampshire. Exeter is a small town of 21,000 souls. It is home to the famous boarding high school, Phillips Exeter Academy. The Academy has about 1,000 students who come from all over the world. It was established in 1781 and has classes that are no larger than twelve students. The Academy utilizes a system where the students sit at a table with their instructor so they get all their questions quickly answered. The campus is large and beautiful. It puts many college campuses to shame. This is accomplished by a billion-dollar endowment and an enrollment fee of just under $50,000 a year. The town was the birthplace of the Republican Party. Both Abe Lincoln and George Washington stayed here. The residents, however, like to think of themselves as being very liberal and they seem to be of that persuasion. The business district is marked by mostly red brick buildings that look like they are straight out of the early part of the 1900's.

In case you are wondering I am a relatively

young 83 and Janice Wayne my child bride is 7 years younger. My cardiologist once said to us, *he is old, you are not*.

Typically, an ordinary workday for me is a boring day. I follow a path through Portsmouth and the surrounding communities searching for typewriters. I buy them at antiques shops, yard and garage sales and other locations. I sometimes find them at places like Goodwill and the Salvation Army. I see people searching through the used clothing racks at these two places, and it makes me wonder how such a wealthy nation can leave so many people in such dire financial condition that they must rely on used clothing.

I buy typewriters for my shop in any condition, including those that I know that I will scrap for parts. For example, most typewriters are full of very small machine screws that are just about impossible to buy today. I save them and any other useful parts, such as platens and nickel-plated parts. I only junk machines that I cannot repair. It is not my intention to turn this into a tutorial on typewriters but it is, after all, a mystery about a typewriter so you need to understand some basic facts about the machines. Namely what I do to find, repair and sell them. So, excuse me if I do go on a little too long.

To a limited extent, I keep a collection of

typewriters at home. The most valuable of these is The Million Dollar Typewriter (MDTW), which I will introduce to you in a little bit. I also have an 1896 Blickensderfer which I consider to be the most ingenious machine of its time or any other time. Contrary to what you might think, it was not of foreign origin but was made in Stamford, Connecticut. It was named after the inventor. He might have lasted longer in business had he named the machine "Jones," or even "Smith." The machine had interchangeable type fonts much like the IBM that came along 100 years later. It did not use a ribbon. Rather, when a key was depressed, the striker swiped an ink pad on its way to the paper. Speaking of the keys, Blickensderfer did some research and found that a typist could type much faster if the keyboard was arranged with the most frequently used keys placed in the center of the keyboard, so he produced a model with this arrangement. As a sop to the rest of the industry, he also offered a model with the standard and slower "QWERTY" arrangement which we are all now stuck with on our computers and cell phones. What might have been!

CHAPTER III – A UNIQUE MACHINE

I digress again, so back to the story of The Million Dollar Typewriter. I do not know exactly what this machine is worth for a host of reasons. The prime determinant relates to whether certain documents were typed on the machine. What I know for certain is that this 1914 Underwood typewriter was located at the Columbia University Physics Laboratory of Enrico Fermi during the Second World War. I know this for sure because there is a tag firmly affixed to the side of the typewriter that says it is the property of the Lab and owned by the U.S. Navy.

Fermi got out of Italy prior to the war (lucky for us) with his Jewish wife. He led the race with Germany to develop atomic weapons and, of course, he won. I believe he single-handedly is responsible for saving the free world from the Nazis. But how many people now even recognize his name?

The original letter to President Roosevelt that bore Albert Einstein's signature was, in fact, written by Fermi. He presented Einstein with two different versions of the letter. Einstein picked one and signed it. It is still hard for me to believe that Einstein was a pacifist, and aside from signing the letter, he gave virtually no support to the research that led to the project. Einstein went off to his comfortable office at Princeton and refused to help with the development of the bomb.

Fermi effectively used Einstein's fame to get President Roosevelt's attention. Thankfully it worked and Government funds became available for Fermi's Lab. The U.S. Navy sponsored the project because the original thinking was that if Germany did develop the weapon first, it would be delivered to our homeland via a port facility.

Now, a word about the documents that could make this typewriter extremely valuable. If I could have documented that the original Roosevelt letter was typed on this machine, it would be worth many millions. One way to accomplish this would be to identify a peculiarity on the typewriter's strikers that could be matched to an impression on the Roosevelt letter. I did a crude forensic examination and could not find any such match. Another problem was the process of trying to place the typewriter at the lab when we know the letter was typed (i.e. 1939). There is a database, run by volunteers, that relates typewriter serial numbers (which are stamped on the machine) to year of production and this data bank says that The Million Dollar Typewriter was produced in 1914. Although this data source is subject to error, it is generally accepted in the trade. It is the best database we have. I was not inclined to accept this as the gospel, since I had acquired a model of one machine from a major American manufacturer that did not even appear in the data bank at all. In other words, it simply did not exist although I owned one of them. In any event, we know for sure that the typewriter was at Fermi's lab during the war and many important documents were undoubtedly typed on it. So, there I was with a very valuable machine that was too large for a safety deposit box, too valuable to store in my closet, too valuable to bury in a hole in the ground or a cabin in the woods. It was too valuable to publicize, so naturally I kept it quiet. At some point in the future I was sure that I would want to try and sell it. That would be when I thought I knew as much about the machine as I could ever learn. I kept the MDTW at home in a large box close to the other machines in my private collection.

CHAPTER IV - AN OFFER, OR A DEMAND?

I need to explain how the MDTW came into my possession. A couple of years ago, I got a telephone call from a woman who lived in northern Massachusetts. More about that later. At that time, I knew nothing about the machine except that it was in Fermi's Lab during WWII. It stays in my closet at home for a month or so. I think no more about it until one morning, a nicely dressed gentleman comes into the shop.

"Good morning, sir. How can I help you?"

He speaks with a decidedly German accent.

"I understand that you have recently purchased a 1914 Underwood typewriter from a young man who is a student at Columbia University. I would like to buy it. I am prepared to offer you a fair price for it. May I see it now?"

The words are politely spoken but they strike me as more like a command as opposed to an offer. Bessie and Aaron did not raise a dummy. I reason that with someone so eager to buy the machine that there must be something about it that I do not know.

"You could certainly look at it if were here. But it's not. Perhaps, you could come by in a few days and I will arrange to have it here for you to inspect."

"We are in town only briefly so speed is of the utmost. Can you have it here this afternoon?"

He said it more like a demand than a question! And I think to myself who is the "WE" he just mentioned?

"No, I am alone in the shop as you can see. However, I can try to have it here sometime tomorrow, if that works for you. Perhaps you could get a nice room at the Exeter Inn. I can call you tomorrow when the typewriter is here."

"No need for that. We will be staying in our jet airplane tonight. I will be here when you open, tomorrow morning."

There is the "WE" again. So, he at least has a pilot with him. And again, it comes out like an order. He flies here on a plane to buy the typewriter that only three people know I have. I wonder how he knows I have it. How strange is that? His plane is a jet. Is that supposed to impress me?

"OK, see you then."

No good-by, no thank you or anything else. He simply wheels around in a decidedly military manner and leaves. I'm not thinking too clearly at this point but my guts tell me I am not in a good situation. I do what I always do when confronted with such a situation. I put a closed sign in the window and head home to tap the best brain in the family. Janice, of course.

As I walk in the door, she says, "Hey, what did you do to get home so early? Didn't sell the entire shop, did you?"

"Well no, but I apparently made one sale that puzzles the life out of me. Tell me what you think of this." I give her a detailed account of the early morning visitor.

"Well, what's wrong with selling a typewriter? Isn't that why you have a shop? How much did he offer for the MDTW?"

"We didn't get that far. Besides, that's almost irrelevant. What I'm really concerned about is how he knew about the machine and how did he know I had it?"

"I see your point. He must know something about the machine that you don't. You said he came here by jet?"

"He did, presumably a jet of his own. I wish I knew some more about that guy. Maybe I'm all wet and he is just a big-time collector like Tom Hanks or Nicolas Cage."

"If he came by airplane, why don't you call your friend Josh at the airport? Maybe he can tell you something about where your customer came from."

"Aha. That's why I came to talk to you. Thanks. I am going to run out to Pease now and talk to Josh."

I have known Josh for some time. I met him in Tallahassee, Florida where I was a student pilot and he operated the tower at the local airport. This is how I got to meet him for the first time. I was practicing landings and takeoffs one Sunday morning. I didn't venture away from the airport as I usually did because there was a storm front moving in. I was the first one to fly the Aeronca Champ after a 400-hour overhaul. My instructions from the airport owner was to warm up the engine thoroughly before I took off to make sure that the engine was operating properly after the overhaul. I followed his instructions to the letter. As I was flying the downwind leg of my 3rd landing, I noticed an AF Jet flying a straight-in landing approach. The Air Force based nearby at Tyndall Airforce Base used the Tallahassee Airport to practice instrument approaches. They never actually landed, just flew down the runway at a very low altitude. I decided to extend my downwind leg and land after the jet passed by. My altitude was 800 feet. When the jet passed the runway I turned in my base leg (i.e. a left turn to get over to the runway). I cut back on the throttle and as I did, the engine totally quit on me. After what seemed like ten minutes of terror, I finally turned into the runway and prayed that I had enough altitude to reach the runway. I was in a totally abnormal pattern, a long way from the end of the runway. When the terror subsided, I flattened out my glide angle so I could get as much distance out of the plane as possible while at the same time avoiding a stall which would have been fatal. For those of you unfamiliar with these old planes, they do not have an electric starter, so I couldn't try to restart the engine. I also did not have a radio, like most small planes of that era, so I couldn't call the tower to see if there were any other jets following behind me. All the way down I kept looking for a green light from the tower to signify that it was ok to land. Never got it. All this transpired on my 10th hour of training and only my 2nd solo hour. I made the runway with about 50 feet to spare. Lucky me. Just after I came to a stop and was pushing the plane off to the side of the runway, the owner arrived and started accusing me of failing to apply the carburetor heat to prevent icing. He checked the instrument panel and found that I had indeed applied the carburetor heat. This calmed him down but then he got into one of the seats in the plane and made me go for a ride with him. He tried everything he could to make the engine stall, but it wouldn't. When we got back to the airport, I went up to the tower and met Josh. When I asked him why he never gave me the green light to land, he explained that he knew I was inexperienced and was afraid to confuse me. A weak answer if you ask me. I figured that Josh would remember this, so I went out to the former Pease Airforce Base in Portsmouth, where he was now the manager. He owed me one, didn't he?

"Good morning Josh. It's good to see that you are still running these aircraft safely in and out of the airport. Given the great variety of these planes in terms of size and speed, it seems to me almost a miracle that you don't have at least one collision every week. You must be doing something right."

"Lord I already feel like you are buttering me up so you must need something. Yes? And by the way good morning to you too."

"I'm just stopping by to see an old friend. Now that you mention it however, there is one small favor that you can do for me. After all you have owed me one for many years, haven't you?"

"I knew it. Yes. I suppose I do owe you a small favor for not giving you the green light so long ago. After this just remember it when I bring you some old typewriters to buy because then we will be even."

"You mean you have some typewriters to sell me? Those low-tech devices from a high-tech guy?"

"I have no idea just now. Just remember, we will be even."

"Sure. What I want now is very simple. I had a visitor to my shop today who was strangely familiar with a somewhat valuable typewriter that I own. He wanted to buy it and all but commanded me to get it in the shop by tomorrow morning. This a machine that was in Enrico Fermi's laboratory during World War II."

"Excuse me for interrupting, but what's so strange about him wanting to buy a typewriter? Isn't that what you sell in that typewriter shop of yours?"

"Josh, I have had this machine in my collection for some time. I have no idea how he knew the machine existed, since I have not made any effort to sell or publicize it. Given that, how the hell did he know that I had it?"

"That is very strange indeed."

"What's even stranger is that I got very bad vibes from the guy. He told me he arrived by private jet just this morning so I figured you probably had some contact with him."

"Wait a minute. Is this guy about 6 feet tall and does he speak with a strong German accent?"

"That's him. I knew he must have landed here."

"Not him. Them. There are three of them and they checked in early this morning. They came in on that Learjet, sitting over there by the large hanger. First thing they did was to ask how to get to your shop. Let's go chat with them."

"No way, Josh. The negative vibes I get from their leader are just too strong. And I don't want you to go anywhere near them unless it involves part of your job as manager of the airport. What else do you already know about them?"

"I have their registration number and they have already filed a flight plan to leave here tomorrow morning. So they would appear to be confident their business here would be done by then. I assume said business with you is the only reason they are here."

"The cost of flying a private jet with three passengers here, even from New York would hardly be equivalent to the value of a normal typewriter. Particularly since it has not been advertised for sale."

"New York, my foot. The flight plan says their origin was Buenos Aires, Argentina."

"Now I really wouldn't go anywhere near them. We all know that Argentina was a favorite destination for Nazis escaping the crumbling ruins of Germany at the end of WWII."

"Maybe you are putting two and two together and getting five, Murray."

"Maybe so, but I am unwilling to bet the farm on it."

"What arrangement do you have to transfer the typewriter to them?"

"Well, none really, but the leader is supposed to show up the first thing tomorrow morning, expecting to buy the machine for what he thinks is a fair price. Whatever that might be."

"Why not just sell the damn typewriter to him for $50,000 and pocket the cash?"

"That sounds simple. I agree. But if the typewriter is worth that much money to him plus the expense of flying all that way to get it, then it must be worth a lot more. Who knows why? Don't think that I am paranoid. If that crew is as evil as I think they might be they probably will not leave any 'loose ends' around. I would just as soon not be a 'loose end.'"

"Murray, you will pardon me but that *does* seem a bit paranoid. Why don't you just report the creep to the police?"

"Josh, flying here from Argentina to buy a typewriter is not a crime and you know the cops would laugh me out of the station. And rightly so."

"You're right. What are you going to do, then?"

"Josh. What am I going to do? I hadn't thought about it until just now. On the basis of what you have told me about their origin in Buenos Aries and their plan to leave tomorrow, I think I will quietly slip out of town for an overdue vacation."

"Where will you go?"

"I think it is safer for both of us if you don't know. In fact, I really don't know yet.

"I am going to get us some throwaway cell phones in case we need to talk. I'll be back in a while. In the meantime, stay away from that plane and watch your back."

I drive to Lowes and buy three throw away cells and return to the base. When I get there, I approach Josh's tower with care. Once I can see that the bad guys are not nearby, I go up to the tower and give Josh one of the cells.

"Murray, I'm beginning to wonder if I shouldn't take a vacation myself."

"Josh. Do what you need to do to take care of yourself, but since you don't know where I am going, I don't think you are in any danger. On second thought, perhaps you can help them start after me. A false lead. You could tell them I talked about a vacation in Miami which is plausible because both Janice and I have ties there."

"I don't know about that. If these guys are as dangerous as you think they are, I'd sooner have nothing at all to do with them."

"Okay, but I just decided that we would head for Miami, so you can tell them or not as you see fit. If you learn anything at all about them that you feel would be helpful to me, I'd appreciate a call. Just don't take any chances. I hope to see you soon.

"I may be making a mountain out of the proverbial mole hill but my instincts tell me to get out of town as quickly as I can. Like tonight. Since I have an appointment with them tomorrow morning to sell them the typewriter I don't think they will be watching me. Good luck, Josh. I will be in touch as soon I can make any sense out of all this. None of this would have happened were it not for my stupid typewriter. However long it takes I will make up for any losses that you take."

"Hey. Like you said at the beginning I owe you one so don't worry about it. Take good care of yourself and Janice. I'll see you later."

"Later."

CHAPTER V - WE LEAVE TOWN

I drive back home and tell Janice about the morning's events.

"I don't like the feel of this situation and I think we need to get out of here tonight," she says.

"I go along with that but how do we do that?"

"Why don't we put you in charge of this entire expedition since you're thinking like an experienced tactician, whereas I am not thinking at all? We can't travel under our own names obviously. That means we need to have phony driver's licenses and maybe other ID papers. Do you know anyone who can produce such documents?"

"Well no, I don't, but I know someone who just might."

"And who might that be?"

"You don't know him. I knew him a long time ago and I don't believe you ever met him."

"Somebody out of your shady past, huh?"

"Not really. Just an acquaintance who ran a company that dealt close to the line and over the line now and then. If he is still around he just might know where to go. I'll get his number and call him."

"Hi Barry. This is Murray Segal. Long time no see. I'm good and you? Listen, I have a problem you might be able to help me with. Do you still live in North Hampton and could I stop by in a about 30 minutes.? Well, I'd rather not talk on the phone. Ok to stop by?"

I drive to his house immediately.

"C'mon in. What's so important that made you rush over here like this?"

"Barry. I need some phony ID papers and I thought you might know somebody who could produce them in a hurry."

"What's going on?"

"I'd rather not say. Can you help?"

"Sure. The guy's name is Joe Fletcher. He runs a small print shop on Lincoln Street in Exeter as cover-up for his real source of income, which is forgery. He has a hidden stairway in the rear of the print shop which leads upstairs to the lab where he does the usual fake ID papers such as driver licenses, wills, passports and anything else he can sell. Just call him and make sure you let him know that you are aware of his forgery shop. Don't know whether you need any more papers but he can fake just about anything."

Barry gives me the telephone number and I return home and call Fletcher when I get there.

"Is this Joe Fletcher?"

"It is but this is a business phone and the shop is closed for the day." A grumpy answer. He slams the phone down without giving me a chance to say anything. I call back immediately and when he answers, I say, "Don't hang up, I need a rush job done and I am willing to pay a reasonable premium to get it done immediately."

"You mean tonight?"

"I do. It is essential that I get two driver's licenses and passports tonight."

"Let's talk about that at my print shop. Come on over and knock on the door. The lights will be off but I will be waiting and will let you right in."

"OK. See you in five minutes. I am right around the corner."

When I do enter his shop, I am looking at a frail older man who appears to be in his sixties, sporting a beard and moustache. I shake his hand and he leads me into the print shop and sits me down at a desk in the reception area close to the front door.

"I prefer to talk with you in a less public place where we can't be seen through your window. Let's go upstairs to your lab and work things out in complete privacy."

He winces a bit at the mention of his upstairs forgery lab. I purposely mention the lab to let him know that I am aware of it. Besides I do want to get away from the window. He shuts off the light and leads me up the stairs into the windowless lab. It has a photo setup, a small printing press and other devices that I cannot identify.

"Quite a set-up you have here and barely a half mile from the police station." I put a knowing look on my face to imply that I am not above squealing on him if he tries to screw me.

"I need two driver's licenses, one for me and one for my wife. And two passports as well. She is standing by at home and could be here in just 5 minutes after I call her. How much will this cost us?"

"My normal charge for a license and passport is $2500 but given the rush, it will cost you $10,000 for the pair."

"I can't afford that much."

"Take it or leave it."

I call his bluff, stand up and walk back

toward door at the top of the stairs.

"Wait. Since you are already here and I can get the job done this evening, I will accept $7,500 for the documents."

"Make it $6,000 and we have a deal."

"Deal. Of course, it must be paid in cash and there will be no receipt."

"I understand Let's go to work on me and I will call my wife to come on over with the cash when you are ready for her."

Wow. He decides to trust me for five minutes and he sets me right down in front of the camera and begins to work. Fortunately, I anticipated the need for cash and closed our checking and savings accounts earlier in the day.

"Jan. Come on over to the shop and bring $6,000 with you. Hide the rest of the cash at home."

"OK. See you in a few minutes."

Punctuality is not generally one of Jan's attributes but this time she shows up just six minutes later. This tells me she is feeling the seriousness of our situation. Fletcher takes the photos he needs and lets us know it will take him about two hours to complete the work. I give him $3,000 and promise the balance when I pick the licenses up in two hours. I made up our new names, Harry and Silvia Stein because I think my roman nose would give me away if I used Jones or Smith.

It's a good idea to hedge your bets when dealing with a crook. Not that I have dealt with many crooks but I do watch TV, go to the movies and read many mystery stories on my Kindle.

We leave Fletcher to his work and go on back to the house.

"Jan, we need to figure out how we are going to get out of town quietly without letting anyone see us."

"Are you sure that's the smart thing to do? Perhaps we can create a diversion of some sort that sends these guys looking for us in an area that is as far from where we go as possible."

"Like what kind of a diversion? Did you have something specific in mind?"

"The first idea that pops into my mind is to get a couple to take some airplane tickets to Miami that we buy with our real names on them. We give them the tickets for free with the proviso that they use them and save their own tickets to use another time. I don't like this too much because we would have to trust the couple to use our tickets first. In this situation, it is best if we don't trust anyone but ourselves.

Another idea would be to drive our car to Portland where we will leave it at the airport. We buy two tickets under our own names and get on a plane to Miami. When we get there, we get on a return flight but use our phony ID's for the tickets. When we get back to Portland, we leave our car parked at the airport. We rent or buy another car. Then we head north. We will have plenty of time to decide exactly where we will end up."

"I like that plan but there is one key part to work out. Renting a car would probably be impossible because of all the information the rental car companies require. Buying a car is feasible but it drains our cash substantially and we would have the problem of registration and insurance. I suppose we might find a shady auto dealer who would do the registration and insurance for us for the right price. I don't see any other alternative. We are already on the wrong side of the law so why not go all in? I think we should try that scheme. I will go back to Fletcher's now and pick up our drivers' licenses."

I doubt that we are being watched. To be sure, I take a devious and roundabout route to Fletcher's shop. I see no sign that I am being followed, but as a final precaution, I park a block away and walk the rest of the way to his shop. More stuff I have learned from reading mystery novels. This would be almost comical but it is so real to me that I shake a bit as I walk the final few steps. He opens the door after a couple of light taps and I slip quickly inside.

"I have taken every precaution to make sure that no one has seen me come here. Just in case, get me the negatives and plates that you used. I will destroy them on my way out of town. For your safety as well as mine, I don't want anyone to connect the two of us."

"I appreciate that. Before I get them, did you bring the balance that you owe me?"

This guy has been around the block once or twice and knows all the angles. I suppose it pays a thief to trust no one. I hand over the 30 one hundred dollar bills. He selects three at random and then tests them to make sure they aren't counterfeit. After handing me the new licenses and passports he goes back to the outer door, opens it, looks out carefully and motions me to leave. No thank you. No good luck. Nothing, not even a smile. I, too, skip the thank you and get out of there as quickly as I can. I don't encounter anyone on the walk back to the car or the drive home.

"Have a look at your new driver's license and passport Janice, um I mean Silvia."

"OK. Let's get our carry-on bags and get out of here while the getting is good."

We carry our bags and the MDTW (in a box) out to the Saab and drive away carefully.

"I didn't see anyone suspicious, Silvia. Did you?"

"No, I didn't see anyone at all."

We follow our plan and take I-95 north to Portland. It is late when we arrive so we register at a motel near the airport under our real names. It is our plan to take a flight to Miami with our real ID's and then a return flight to Portland under our phony ID's. Our thinking is that the bad guys will be able to locate the Saab, which we will leave for them at the Portland airport, and then track us through the airline to Miami. Knowing that both of us had historical ties to that area they will look for us there. I went to the University of Miami and Jan spent much of her childhood there where her family lived. After we land in Miami we will return to Portland under our false ID's and leave the Saab parked at the airport. We are hoping that this diversion works without a flaw. Ideally the bad guys will be searching for us in Florida while we are heading northward from Portland looking for a good place to light. Now comes the risky part of our plan. We need wheels. The only way we figure that we can obtain them is to find a slightly shady auto dealer who would do the registration and insurance for us. For a fee, of course. We board a flight to Miami with our real names and then a late return flight to Portland as Harry and Silvia Stein. It is late by the time we get back so we take a room at a motel near the airport and flop into bed, exhausted. Sleep is instantaneous.

After breakfast, we drive around Portland in the Saab and after a lot of searching we find a likely used car lot. By likely looking, I mean the cars on the lot are all well used and the place looks sort of run down. A sign at the entrance to the lot announces that we are about to enter Sam's Used Car Lot. We don't stop because I don't want the proprietor to see the Saab. We park a block away and walk back to the lot.

"Silvia, this is where you must be your usual charming self. Also, have a bundle of those 100-dollar bills ready."

Of all the heaps on the lot, a late model Mazda 6 looks like the best bet. As we walk onto the lot, a jolly looking fellow that I take to be the owner pops out of a little building in the middle of the lot and approaches us with his hand extended.

"Hi, my name is Sam and I am the owner of this emporium. What can I do for you today?"

He is a jovial, slightly rotund fellow, almost a caricature of your friendly automobile dealer.

"Hello yourself. My name is Harry Stein and this is my wife Silvia. We are looking for a car that we can buy and get on the road quickly. That Mazda 6 looks interesting. Could we have a look?"

"Certainly. A good choice. Maybe, the best bargain here. Only about 20,000 miles on it and it can be yours for only $12,000."

The car has some body rust here and there but I'm thinking that is a good sign because old Sam has not tried to hide it with some filler.

"This might work." I try to be very casual in my response. "Can we take it for a test drive?"

"Sure. You can take it for as long as you like. Try it out thoroughly."

"Well about an hour or less is all I need."

"Good. May I see your driver's license?"

"Sure," as I hand him the Harry Stein version of my license.

"Ah. A member of my tribe. Nice to meet you Harry."

He hands me the license back and flips me the keys. Silvia and I get in and start the engine. Sam waves to us as we leave the lot and head toward the Interstate. It started easily and runs smoothly. I stay just below the 65-mph speed limit on the Interstate. Everything appears to work well including the steering, the brakes, the windshield washers. There is no unusual noise from the exhaust system and all the instruments work. The interior is clean and well cared for.

"Silvia, I think this car fits our needs perfectly and now the only problem is how to get Sam to take care of the registration and insurance."

"Why don't we ask him to rent the car to us on a long-term basis, say six months, so then he takes care of the insurance and registration?"

"That's a great idea. He will probably charge us an arm and two legs to do this but that's the only way I can see to get past the registration and insurance barriers and get the car on the road. You are so smart. You will make a great thief."

We drive back to the lot and tell Sam what we want and surprisingly he will do it.

"I think I will need about $700 a month to

cover that with six months due in advance."

"That's a lot and I don't know if we can handle it."

"If you will pay for all the regular maintenance on the car and any repairs necessary, I can get the cost down to $500 per month. That would also carry a mileage limitation of 1,000 miles per month."

"We have a deal. We would like to get on the road this afternoon. Any problem with that?"

"No problem at all. In fact, if you come inside you can have the car right now."

"Great. Let's do it."

He is as good as his word. We are out the door in 30 minutes. I drive the Mazda to our Saab and Sylvia follows me with it to the airport where I leave it in the long-term lot. I took the precaution of saving the original parking ticket. The Saab has been my favorite car for years and Gary, Adam and Tony have kept it running smoothly. I leave the ticket in the car and dispose of the new one. We both are very tired after the events of the past few days so we agree to stop over for a day. Silvia gets out our new AAA TourBook and decides we will stay at the Motel 8 in Freeport, the home of LL Bean's home store.

"If we stay around Freeport we can load up

on winter clothing that we will probably need up there in the north country."

"Sounds good to me because it means that we can stop at Barnacle Billy's at Perkins Cove for some lobster. It probably will be some time before we see a lobster again."

"It's good to see that the danger we are feeling has not distracted you from your appetite."

"Hey. First things first."

It is a short drive up Route 1 to Ogunquit and Perkins Cove. Ogunquit means "Beautiful Place by the Sea" and that most certainly describes Perkins Cove.

"This would be a perfect place to land, all other things being equal, but if the Nazis ever followed us here we would be trapped unless we could swim to London. I don't know about you but I don't think I could make it. I left my water wings back at home."

"Funnyman. But that does raise the question about what kind of a place we are looking for. Perkins Cove is just ahead so maybe we could talk about that during lunch if it wouldn't distract you from the lobster."

"Silvia, nothing will distract me from lobster. That's a question we should answer though before we leave here so we don't go wandering aimlessly. Let's go in and get a table outside where we can eat and scheme at the same time."

I order two 1 pound lobsters for me and a lobster roll with no mayo for Silvia. You should begin to see why she maintains here svelte figure. It is a glorious day on the deck. Too bad it wouldn't be a practical place to stay.

While we eat, we begin to noodle about a plan to stay well away from the bad guys.

"I think the most important attribute for a place to land would be that it offers a variety of escape routes if the Nazis get close. That means no place on the seacoast will do. And that means we head north a least as far as the Augusta area. You know dear lady that early in my career I did a lot of consulting work for the Maine State Highway Commission which turned into their present Department of Transportation (DOT). During that part of my career I travelled every mile of Maine's primary highway system from Kittery in the south to Fort Kent and Allagash in the north. This gives me a feel for the state even though that was some time ago. We also need to remember that this trip may very well be a two-week vacation but it certainly could turn into a much longer stay away from home. Given our dwindling cash stash, we likely would have to find jobs to sustain us."

"Oh no. Do you really expect that to happen? Will we be away that long?"

"Silvia, I don't really know what to expect but what is that old saying? Plan for the worst and hope for the best. It strikes me that it would be prudent to find a place to live and plan that we might be there for six months to a year. To me all signs point to Maine's northern most reaches otherwise known as Aroostook County, the potato capital of the east coast."

"Oh my, that sounds like a perfectly dreadful place to live even for just a month."

"Hey snob, why don't you nose into your trusty AAA TourBook which should tell you something about that area. I might be able to fill in the blanks, here and there."

"OK. Aroostook means Beautiful River. But that's about all I get from the TourBook except names and telephone numbers of restaurants and motels. Let me crank up the Toshiba and see what I can learn about the county. Ok. The land area of Aroostook is just shy of 6,700 square miles which makes it the largest county east of the Rocky Mountains. In other words, it is huge. In 2015, there were about 68,000 people living there. Which is fewer than lived there in 2012. So, it is shrinking. That's about ten people per square mile and that dear husband is tiny. Particularly when you deduct the population living in the few largest cities and towns. In other words, there are large areas of land where almost nobody lives."

"It's beginning to sound like a place where I neither want to live nor to visit. But it can't be that bad, can it? What's the population of Presque Isle?"

"It says here about 9,200 folks. That makes it about half the size of Exeter. The median house value in the county is about $92,000 and the median rent is $557 per month. If you hadn't heard, it is known for the potato crop. They actually close the schools when harvesting time rolls around so the kids can help work in the fields."

"I don't believe that I will be much interested in potato farming. Tell me some good attributes of the area."

"Caribou is the second largest city with about 8,200 people. Presque Isle is the home of several colleges including a branch of the State University. It has a weekly newspaper, the *Star-Herald*, no TV stations but several radio stations."

"Stop right there. I'm guessing that if we

decide to head for 'The County,' we should aim
for the Presque Isle/Caribou area. Isn't there a
third town called Fort Fairfield to the east of
Presque Isle that lies close to the Canadian
Border? It seems like I was there a long time
ago."

"What a memory. I knew you could
remember other things besides places to eat!"

"Very funny," I respond with a grunt and a
sour look.

"Oh, lighten up, loveman and forget about
having the last word with me. You are
overmatched."

Truer words were never spoken so I remain
silent.

"Presque Isle is also home to the Aroostook
Centre Shopping Mall and the Northern Maine
Regional airport is nearby."

"Silvia, Presque Isle is almost as far away
from Miami as you can get. Are we agreed that
we should focus on it as a place to land?"

"I don't have a better idea, so yeah, I agree."

"Good. Now, let's get on to L.L. Bean in
Freeport and stock up on warm clothing. You
want to drive?"

"I do. It will keep my mind from wandering
to the predicament that we are in."

"When we near Freeport, I will lead you to

their main store which is open 24 hours a day. There is also an outlet store nearby and maybe we should go there first."

CHAPTER VI - NORTHWARD

We follow Interstate 295 northward to the Freeport, Maine area and then get onto U. S. Route 1 which leads us directly to Bean's Outlet Store.

"Your expert navigator has safely gotten us to Bean's. Has the drive tamped down your misgivings about our situation?"

"It kind of has. At least for the time being. Bring some cash and let's go get some clothes."

It takes me about 20 minutes to buy everything I need to keep warm this winter, even in the coldest of climes. On the other hand, it takes Silvia some 2 hours to do the same job for herself.

As we check out and walk to the car, it is approaching lunch time. The Toshiba recommends that we eat at The Tuscan Brick Oven Bistro which is just a few blocks north on Route 1. We eat a leisurely lunch.

"Silvia, it feels like we are deliberately trying to delay getting on the road, doesn't it?"

"To be perfectly honest with you, it is

deliberate on my part."

"I guessed as much. I have an idea. It's close to one thirty now. Why don't we find a motel and spend the rest of the day here? We can loaf, read some, watch a movie or two and maybe even fool around a little. That way we can start out fresh early tomorrow morning."

"I like the sound of that so long as I get to choose at least one movie."

Our tastes in movies radically differ. I like mystery and film noir types while Silvia likes chick flicks, naturally. I notice she didn't nix the fooling around part. It is a good trade off, one chick flick for a few hours of fooling around. I'll take that swap anytime.

"Don't think I didn't miss the glint in your lascivious eyes."

"I plead guilty as charged. Ask the Toshiba where to stay."

It turns out that there is a Hilton Garden Inn close by and we get there in a matter of minutes. Great place. We splurge on a suite and drag our clothes and the MDTW inside. The place is great. Indoor and outdoor pools and a whirlpool. This is great for Silvia because she likes to swim. My asthmatic lungs limit my swimming dramatically. Just thinking about swimming brings back an ancient memory of my worst swimming escapade. I was a teenager and worked at Sears Park in East Hampton, Connecticut, where I was brought up. I bailed out the rowboats they rented out, cleaned up the leaves and tracked down the occasional lost boat. My swimming was so bad that I used to take a rowboat out into the middle of Lake Pocotopaug, throw down an anchor and jump off the boat to practice swimming. I use the word loosely because swimming was largely dog paddle, maybe a little side stroke. One day I went out there with a boat that turned out to be missing the anchor. I jumped off anyway and when I came to the surface the boat was long gone due to a very heavy wind. First panic. Then I regained my senses and decided to swim to an island in the middle of the lake. It was farther than going back to the shore but that would have been against the wind. I made it to the island and collapsed on the small beach. A few minutes later, Arnold Purple, the owner of the entire island sauntered down from his house. He took one look at me and asked, "Aren't you Aaron Segal's son?"

"Yes sir, I am."

"Well, are you going to swim back to the park or could I take you in my boat?"

He is making a bad joke but I'm too young

and shaken up to notice. "That would be good."

I thought to myself there goes the job at the park and who knows what kind of discipline I would get from my parents. Lucky for me he never told anyone.

"Silvia, one thing that we didn't get at Bean's are swimsuits. This place has two pools and a whirlpool. I don't know if Bean's carries swim suits but I bet they do. Why don't you take the car and get a couple of suits for us while I guard the MDTW and the cash here in the room?"

"Sure. I'll be back in a few minutes."

An hour and a half later, she returned with suits for both of us. We began to undress to put on the suits. Alas we were interrupted by the need to fool around. We didn't get to the pool for another hour, but who's counting? We were in the pool for an hour and a half. Given my challenged swimming style I spent most of the time in the whirlpool, while Silvia divided her time between the two of them. We were too lazy and sated to venture out of the place for dinner but rather sent out for some pizza.

"Silvia, we need to pick out a movie to go along with the pizza. How about *Deadly Affair* with James Mason, Simone Signoret, and Maximillian Schell?"

"Not exactly a chick flick but the world is not

perfect and I'm too tired to think of a film myself. Raise the curtain."

"Let's wait a bit for the pizza."

I barely get the words out of my mouth when there is a knock on the door. I pay for the food and we start the film on Netflix. The end of a perfect day. The movie is fun but I do have some trouble understanding some of the dialogue. Part of the problem is the British accents and part is my ancient ears. Even Silvia has some difficulty with the dialogue, so it's not just me. It is very late when the movie ends. We both take showers to wash off the chlorine from the swimming pool but we are too tired to fool around anymore. The TV news is showing the latest goings on in The Middle East, Syria, Turkey, and Germany. Not a pleasant way to end the day but the world is what it is. We skip the sports because we really don't want to know about the latest struggles of the Red Sox, and their brand new 207 million-dollar pitcher, David Price. We fall into a deep sleep the moment our heads hit the pillows.

Bright and early next morning we have breakfast at the Inn and then take off northward on I-95. Silvia's Toshiba has informed us that it is 270 miles to Presque Isle and it should take us about 4 hours. We could be there by lunch time barring unforeseen happenings, which always happen.

"Is it ok with you if I drive?" I ask Silvia.

"Yeah, I'm not in a driving mood. I'm particularly not interested in driving to Presque Isle, no matter how far it might be from here."

"I know you aren't and neither am I, but we have been through this before and reasoned that it is our best choice. Your negativity is not helping."

"I know. I apologize."

We drive in silence, each thinking of all the places we'd rather be. This has nothing to do with Maine. It's a great state and past visits there have been fun and fruitful. The fact that the Nazis could tracking us down casts a pall over everything else. We stay on I-95 and skirt the westerly most sections of Portland. This is the largest city in Maine with 66,000 residents and a healthy downtown. It is a major port in terms of product because many oil tankers visit the waterfront and unload their crude cargo to a pipeline which goes north all the way to Montreal, Canada. There are lots of things to do here in this vibrant city. Among the most memorable for me is a walking tour around Old Town and a cruise to the harbor islands. Food and drink is plentiful in Old Town as are the lovely tourists from all over the country who fill the bars and restaurants. What memories. Before I met Silvia, of course.

"Hey. Are you still with me?"

Silvia's abrupt question brings me back to the present.

"I'm with you all the way, and back. Would you like to take over the driving for a while?"

"Sure."

I pull off onto the breakdown lane and we quickly change places. This is not a recommended practice. This is a special circumstance and while it is unsafe and probably illegal, it is also the least of our worries.

"Ok captain, take us away from the bad guys."

"You know Harry, I have known fear in my life and I guess you have also but it has always been momentary. This is different and not fun. It's there every minute and it's suffocating."

"I know it. Why don't we just decide to relax and live in the moment. There are no physical facts to suggest we should be fearful."

"You are right and I will do my best. The

weather is cooperating. The day could not be better and the company is the best."

"No truer words were ever spoken."

The miles roll by. We stop for gas after a while. As we approach the capitol city of Augusta, I say to Silvia, "Let's get off at exit 109. You should have a peek at the seat of state government for your new home and besides it will give me a chance to do some more reminiscing."

"You bet. I could do with a break."

Silvia drives off I-95 and onto Western Avenue and just past the interchange is the Senator Hotel and Spa.

"I remember the hotel alright but I don't think there was any Spa back in the day. I remember the bar and countless nights entertaining a few job specific officials."

"Ugh. That sounds like hard work."

"Not really. They were solid technical guys. We solved many problems at that bar and made the world a better place. At least this part of the world."

"Oh, my God. Stop before I throw up."

"Aw. Women. You just don't understand the joy of designing a small-town bypass to take traffic out of a congested downtown."

"Did you do that?"

"Well yes. I did as a matter of fact. In Ogunquit for one. Turns out the local merchants liked their tiny downtown congested. They did not appreciate what we were trying to do for them and rejected the plan."

"Glory be, imagine that. They must have enjoyed the ringing of their cash registers. How quaint and unusual."

"Never mind that stuff. We are here and we can do some sightseeing have lunch and dinner and stay over-night."

"Sounds like a plan to me. I hope I didn't bruise your feelings with the sarcasm."

"Nah, It's just life in the big city. Besides, I am used to it."

We check into the Senator and take all our stuff to the room with some help from a bellman. The MDTW goes on the closet floor and I pile the Bean's clothing on top of it. What could be better than spending the rest of the morning in the Spa followed by a tasty lunch? Not much.

"Come on Silvia, I'll take you to see what little there is to see in this capitol city. It has been my experience that all state capitals are boring places with not much to see."

First, we drive toward the downtown a few

minutes and stop at the impressive capitol building. We decide not to take a tour of the building. Instead we drive around the downtown which is directly on the bank of the Kennebec River. Then it's back to the Inn to partake of more spa time and a few movies.

"Silvia, if you look to your right as we get near the inn you will see the Maine State Airport on a steep rise toward the runway. No fun landing or taking off here. I've done it. What is fun, there are a ton of antique shops south of here where I used to shop frequently, but I'd rather go back to the Inn. More spa time, some movies, dinner and a few drinks and who knows what else."

"Like I couldn't imagine what the 'what else' would be, now could I?"

"Knowing me as you do, you probably can."

We accomplish all the above, and eventually fall into a deep sleep and don't move until nine o'clock the next morning.

"I'm glad we stayed the day here. I feel rested and relaxed compared to the last few days. I'll even take the wheel for a while."

"Good, I charged up the Toshiba at the Senator so I can answer any questions you have when we get on the road."

We do just that and we are in the car, zipping along at 70 mph, a few minutes after 9:00 am. In just a wee bit over one hour we approach the Bangor, Maine area where I-95 abruptly changes direction by swinging straight north. A few miles to the north we pass the exit to the main campus of the University of Maine at Orono. I can feel Silvia getting uptight as we approach Orono. I know she is thinking that this would be a good place to settle so I meet that head on.

"I'd really like to settle here because we both would like the academic environment but there would be limited opportunities in terms of escape routes so I don't think it's wise from a safety standpoint."

"I know. We have been over this several times and you are right. My Toshiba tells me to exit the Interstate here because we can buy a copy of Presque Isle's weekly newspaper here. The paper is owned by a Bangor publishing company. While you are driving, I can be checking up on the local Presque Isle news. It is a way to start familiarizing ourselves with the area."

"Sure."

I get off at the Orono exit and we find a variety store/gas station and buy a copy of the

Presque Isle Star-Herald. When we get back on the Interstate Silvia starts browsing through the newspaper while stopping now and then to bring me up to date.

"Interesting. We should feel right at home. Not only was there a murder very recently but there is a compilation of each of the stops made by every Trooper at Troop F of the State Police. There is an article about a spate of vandalism in the area and a strike by nurses. The school district budget has been vetoed and there is a photo of two guys wrestling in a large container full of mashed potatoes and a contest to see who can eat the most potatoes. HONEST."

"Surely you must be pulling my leg."

"Don't call me Shirley and I am not pulling your leg."

I drive the next leg of our trip to Houlton, Maine where I-95 ends at the Canadian border.

As we near the outskirts of the city, Sam's wonderful car starts to run very rough.

"Jeez, Silvia, do you feel that?"

"Of course, I do. It feels like this car is on its last legs. Broken legs at that. What do we do?"

"We are going to find a repair shop and let a mechanic look at it."

We make it to a Sears which has an automotive shop and pull into the parking lot.

The manager lets me know that all his mechanics are currently flat out and he may or may not get one to look at the car by the end of the day.

"We are just passing through. Based on what you are telling me, we should probably find a place tonight. Am I reading you, right?"

"That would be wise, particularly if the car needs parts that we don't have in stock. I would recommend the Shiretown Inn and Suite. It is a good place to stay, with a pool and it's not very far from here. We could call you a taxi but it would be faster for you to wait a few minutes and I'll have one of our men run you over there."

Five minutes later a giant of man comes into the waiting room and introduces himself.

"Hi, my name is Moose. I can drive you over to the Shiretown right now."

"Good to meet you, Moose. My name is Harry and this is my wife, Silvia. I'll have to get some stuff from our car."

"Sure. I will get my car and park near you so we can load up."

He pulls up a couple of minutes later in a very old Buick Station Wagon. It looks like a relic from a couple of decades ago and carries the scars and rust to prove it.

"This looks like a classic, Moose."

If I am to become proficient with the lies, I need to practice, practice. Practice.

"It needs a bit of body work but it runs like a top."

Needs a full body transplant, that's what I think to myself. I catch a bit of a snicker from Silvia but fortunately Moose is busy transferring our suit cases and doesn't hear her. It is a short drive to the Shiretown and the old Buick does run very smoothly. At the desk the desk clerk tells us that they do have a few rooms for the night.

"Our car broke down and it is possible we may stay more than one night so put us down for two nights."

"Certainly sir. May I see you driver's license and a credit card?"

"We will be paying with cash. I don't use credit cards."

"Not many people use cash these days. We have a nice room available at $129.00 per night. Since you don't know if you will be with us the second night a one-night deposit will do."

I pay the bill and we push a luggage rack out to the car. Moose helps us load it up. When we finish, he looks at me and asks, "Is there anything else I can help you with?"

"Actually, there is. Could you pick us up at dinner time and join us for dinner?"

"I can certainly pick you up but dinner is not necessary."

"Well it's not necessary but we would be delighted if you could join us. We are strangers to this town and are totally unfamiliar with it. I'm sure that you could help us out in getting familiar with the area."

"I've lived here all my life and that I could do. I get out of work a five and need about an hour to go home and clean up. Does six o'clock work for you?"

"It does. See you then."

Moose shows up right on time. I remember we still must do some searching of the MDTW to see if we can get any clues as to why the Nazis want it. We can't do it until we get to a place where we have some extended time to work on it. When we get into the Classic Buick, I say to Moose, "Moose, I need to make some repairs on an old typewriter and I wonder if there is a good place to buy some small tools."

Silvia kicks me in the shin and I get the message loud and clear. I have blurted out the word typewriter when it is supposed to be a secret. Thinking quickly, I concoct another lie to cover up this gaff.

"Moose. Please keep this secret. We are going to give this typewriter to an old friend and we want to surprise him with it." My, am I getting good at lying or what?

"My lips are sealed. Why don't we stop at Collins Hardware Store to get your tools right now and then go to dinner?"

"Terrific."

At the hardware store we pick out an assortment of small screwdrivers, pliers, some wrenches and cleaning materials. I pay the bill and Moose takes us to The Taste of China Restaurant. The food is remarkably good. During the meal, we chit chat about things going on in the world. Moose's world, however, is largely confined to the area around Houlton and points further north. This is fine because that's what we are interested in learning.

"Moose. Have you lived here long?"

"Born and brought up here in Houlton and never saw the point of leaving it. The air is fresh and clean here, the people are friendly, and I have worked at Sears long enough so that I know my way around the auto shop. Oh yeah, the deer hunting is great in the fall and so is cross country skiing in the winter. I know the best places to fish. There are lots or tourists here in the summer and some of them are interesting. Well, like yourselves. Why would I leave?"

I can't for the life of me think of a reasonable answer to that question so I look at Silvia who has not been her usual effusive self during the meal. She gets the message.

"Moose, do you have a large family here?"

"Nope. Mom and Dad are gone and I have no brothers or sisters. I have an uncle up near Caribou. I go up there occasionally for a long weekend or vacation."

I make a mental note of this fact. It would be nice to know someone up there but at the same time I don't want to let Moose know that we are headed there.

"What's your uncle's name?"

"Steven Gustafson and he lives in a tiny town called New Sweden."

"Interesting." Nice going Silvia.

I am all talked out at this point so I let out a small yawn and ask Moose to drive us back to the Inn. When we get there, he informs me that the guys at Sears will be bringing our car into the garage first thing tomorrow morning.

"You should know what's going on with it by lunch time if not before. I will call you when we know. Goodnight, and thank you for the dinner."

"Goodnight to you. Silvia and I enjoyed it very much."

When we get inside Silvia goes to the computer and gets a map of New Sweden, Maine and finds out its population is less than 400 people. This may come in handy sometime in the future. I make a note of it, and then we watch a Red Sox game until eleven. I have a beer and Silvia has an iced tea. Another brilliant pitching performance by David Price. He lasts 4 innings and gives up 7 runs before Manager Farrell sends him to the showers. Not bad for a 207 million-dollar mistake. An improvement over his last outing. Breakfast at the Inn and then we wait by the telephone for Moose's call. It comes at 10:30.

"Harry, this is Moose. Do you want the good news first or the bad news?"

"Start with the good news."

"Well we do need a part for your car but it is not expensive."

"And the bad news?"

"We don't have the part in stock so you will be in Houlton one more night."

"The bad news is not so bad. We will survive nicely."

"Will you be needing any rides after work,

today?"

"Probably will but I will call you later and let you know."

I hang up.

"Silvia, we will be spending another night here. We have the rest of the day to do whatever turns you on."

"I am going to see what the Toshiba has to offer. Umm, Trip Advisor mentions Uncle Willy's Candy Shoppe, (with an e). Facebook recommends Grammy's Country Inn, American Restaurant. On Saturday, August 5th there is the Charlie Russell Memorial Jamboree which looks like a carnival. You tube takes us to a Big Truck Stop, The Bridge to Nowhere and various small sculptures. It looks like our choices are limited. We can stay here and watch movies or take a walk which looks pretty boring or do both."

"I must get out of here and get some fresh air. I vote for a walk, lunch at Grammy's Country Inn Restaurant, and then maybe a movie or two. I owe Moose a call first."

So I call.

"Moose. This is Harry Stein. Silvia and I are going out for a walk and lunch. I will let you know later what our plans for tonight are. Maybe we can have dinner."

"Ok. Let me know. "

We walk for a while in the downtown area. There are lots of red brick, rectangular buildings which have a 1940's look about them. Many parking lots which are maybe half full, with a preponderance of pickup trucks. I even spot a vintage 1962 Jeep pickup. I look this one over very carefully and drool a bit. It is model J-2000 in super condition. I don't remember ever seeing one before.

"Stop the wishful thinking Harry. We already have a car and there is no room for any pickup truck."

"Who said I was interested in buying this truck?"

"I read you like a book, loveman, so don't try to snow me."

My good sense says stop right there. She does read me like a book. A comic book. We find a footbridge called the Gateway Bridge just off Main Street. It spans the Meduxnekeag River and leads to a trail on the far side. Neither of us is interested in hiking the trail so we turn around and walk back on the footbridge. After some more walking, we stop at a restaurant called the Courtyard Café on Main Street for lunch. Our waiter tells us that The Courtyard is the only restaurant in Houlton with a full bar.

"That's very interesting. Do you have any Bushmills?"

"Certainly, sir," he informs me, as I wince from Silvia's kick in the shin under the table.

"Well on second thought maybe it is a little early for a drink. I'll just have a Virgil's Crème Soda."

"Yes, sir."

If this guy gives me one more SIR, I will cut his tip in half.

"How many people live in this town?" I ask.

"About 6,000, sir."

There goes his tip.

"If this is the only bar in town, you must have a lot of teetotalers here," I say as I look around the near-empty place.

"We do get very busy, at times, sir."

"Before you get too busy we should order. I'll have a roast beef sandwich, potato salad and iced tea to drink."

"And I'll have a large chef's salad and just water to drink."

"Good choice, madam."

The waiter leaves to place our order in the kitchen. When he is out of hearing, I look at Silvia and utter, "What will you be having for dessert, madam. And will you be bringing anything back for the working girls at the house, madam?"

"Very funny. Your sense of humor grows with each passing day. Grows worse. I hope he didn't hear you. You are already in enough trouble with him."

In a few minutes the waiter comes back with our meals. They are excellent.

"Silvia, thus far our limited dining out experience up here has been surprisingly good."

"Have you ever met a restaurant that you didn't like?"

"Enough. Stop picking on me or I will call Moose right now to come and take you away. It's funny how certain words conjure up images from the past. A long time ago, I had a secretary/office manager who always looked to the dessert menu first and planned the rest of her meal around what she thought she'd have at the end of the meal."

"That would have been Avis. Yes?"

"That's right. I had a small office on Beacon Street in Brookline, Massachusetts, just where the trolley came up from the underground tunnel. We would frequently have lunch across the street at a restaurant called the Elbow Room. I think."

By now I have finished my lunch but Silvia is a slow and careful eater so I wait patiently while she chews her food thoroughly like you are supposed to.

CHAPTER VII - MEET HERMAN BIGGS

Herman Biggs never amounted to much. He was four years old when his dad hit the road, tired of beating up on his wife and Herman, so he went looking for greener pastures. Years later his story came up on every one of the local radio stations and small town weekly newspapers in the area. The greener pastures turned out to be the home of a married woman whose husband took exception to his illicit relationship and beat him to death, along with the wife.

Herman's mom was a loving parent but having to bring up a fatherless son took its toll. She worked long hours six days every week. Her salary as a maid in a local motel barely provided enough money for them to survive on. There were never any of the "extras" of life that most people take for granted. A one-week vacation in the summer and small presents at Christmas and on Herman's birthday. Left alone most of the time while growing up, he took a lot of punishment at school, particularly from the older and bigger kids. He took to carrying a rock for protection and soon learned how to use it as an effective weapon. The other kids caught on and the rock lost its effectiveness. He saw a gun as his only other alternative. He bought a small 22 caliber handgun from the proceeds of odd jobs. Herman's mom knew nothing of these goings on. If she had, she most likely would not been able to do anything about it anyway.

Herman saw the gun as a stepping stone to bigger and better things. At age 15, he started to use his weapon. He saw it as the way to better his life and even to help his mom eventually. It didn't work. He held up a gas station in Exeter and unfortunately the station was equipped with a video monitoring system that allowed the local police to find him within a few hours of the crime. It was easy because they already knew Herman, who had a series of less serious skirmishes with the police. Since he used a gun in the robbery, he drew a long prison sentence is spite of an emotional appeal to the judge by his mother. He drew a ten-year sentence with no possibility of parole for seven years. Herman used the time in prison to develop his skills. He learned many tricks of the trade from his fellow inmates. He also learned much about crime from the guards. In other words, he became a hardened criminal who knew of no legitimate means of earning an income. He studiously avoided any confrontation with the inmates or the guards. He became skilled at deceit and it worked. The parole board granted him the three years off his sentence. He returned to his mother's home to start the next chapter in his life.

He knew the basics of criminal behavior, so it was a natural transition to the life of a private detective. He rented a dingy office and put his name on the door. He did not have a private detective's license and might never get one. He knew the risk of publicly calling himself a private eye without the license so he avoided doing that. He had to develop another method of getting the word out to potential clients who might need an investigator. People from the dark side might need help from someone who knew the ins and outs of crime. He used a network of former prison inmates who had left prison before he did. In turn, they spread the word to other "associates."

The work started to roll in almost immediately. The assignments were mostly small time in nature. Spying on wives or husbands whose mates thought they were cheating. Checking on employees of criminal types who they suspected of having their hands in the till. Nothing big or lucrative but he managed to earn enough to pay the office rent plus some money for his mom to cover some part of his keep at her apartment.

One afternoon Herman is sitting in his office with nothing much to do when there is knock on his door. When he opens the door, a well-dressed man enters. He steps inside without hesitation, as if he has known Herman for a long time and didn't need an invitation.

"Good morning Mr. Biggs. My associates and I are looking for a private detective to undertake a surveillance project for us. You have been recommended to us as the right man for the job."

"Good morning to you. Who was it that did the recommending, if I may ask?"

"That, my good man, is not important. Something you don't need to know."

"Well it's important to me. Specifically, I am not a licensed private detective. I never claimed to be one. If someone is representing me as a licensed PI I want to know who it is so I can straighten him out."

"Herman, we know all about your license problem or should I say lack of a license problem? It is not a problem for us. We will keep your little secret."

His tone has become demanding and authoritative. Almost commanding in nature. It has the desired effect on Herman. He realizes he doesn't know the man's name.

"Pardon me but I don't even know your name yet."

"Of course, you may call me Klaus and my associate out in the car is Hans. When we are finished talking, I will take you outside and introduce you to him."

He talks to me like he is a General and I am a lowly Private.

"We have a job for you. It is well suited to your talents and you will be well paid for the work. It is basically a surveillance project that encompasses a rather broad area around this town with special emphasis on the border crossings between here and Fort Kent on the north and Vanceboro on the south."

"Wow. That's a long stretch of territory with a lot of border crossings. I don't have any employees nor the money to hire any. What would I be looking for? Drugs?"

"No. You would be looking for two individuals who are travelling together and we suspect they may cross the border into

Canada."

"Well why are you looking for them?"

"That is none of your concern but rest assured they are not dangerous. We already know that you have neither the staff nor the resources to do this job right now. It will be your job to hire enough staff to cover the area. You will let us know if the couple crosses the border and where they cross. We suggest a network of cell phones to maintain communications. We will advance you the money necessary to do the job. If they never cross in the area, you get to keep the entire retainer."

"That much territory will require a huge amount of money. Are you sure you want to do this?"

"You will provide us an estimate of the amount for the next 3 months. We have already estimated that the amount will be about $50,000. To be on the safe side and assure a good job we will advance you $150,000. In cash. No questions asked. You get to keep the entire amount regardless whether they cross or not."

The lights go on in Herman's eyes. He has a hard time hiding his emotions. A hundred and fifty thousand dollars will likely leave him with at least half in profit. He contains his emotions but guesses that Klaus knows exactly what is going on in his mind.

"I will get you an estimate by tomorrow but it will take a few days to hire and train the staff necessary to do a good job. I should be able to start to work in about a week."

"Not soon enough. Get it started in 3 days and I will add $25,000 to your fee. Here are a few photographs of the couple you will be looking for. See that every member of the field crew has a copy."

He must think I am very dumb if he must let me know that we need photographs to find the pair we are hunting for.

"You got it. I'll start hiring today and have men on the job. Three days for certain."

"Here is a throw-away cellphone. Call the number I've put on it every day and let me know what's happening."

"OK."

Lord, this was all planned well in advance, he thought to himself. Good thing I didn't give them any kind of a hard time. They would have crushed me like a bug and thrown away the corpse.

Ten minutes later they leave. In another ten minutes, Herman has called six guys he knows and hired them for the project. He also let them know that he needed quite a few additional guys and to spread the word around town. Quietly. Next up, he takes the cash and deposits it in the bank in a new account. The amount of money is too big for a single deposit so he opens two separate accounts so they would draw less attention. The second one was under his mother's name, with him as a cosigner. The job is big enough to convince him that he needs to keep legitimate records and books. Even income taxes. Bummer. The next morning, he calls Klaus on the cell phone to give him a progress report.

"Good morning Klaus. I have hired my best friend to run the field crew and another six are lined up and will start work the day after tomorrow. My friend has started to work this morning and his name is William Jones, really. All the field guys will be taught to cozy up to the border crossing guards. They will report to Bill via cellphone each evening. None of them will know where the money is coming from. I will be treating them as day laborers and paying in cash. Even Bill will not know enough to connect you to the project. Just me. This leaves me free to stay here and supervise or to roam in the field."

"You are turning out to be as good as they

said you were. Very clever. Make sure that they are very careful when cozying up to the border guards. Something like that could blow up quickly, particularly if they are using cash to pay the guards off."

"That's one of the reasons that I will make sure that no one can connect me or you to the project. I got to run. Call you tomorrow."

"OK. I won't hold you up any longer. It appears you have everything in hand."

CHAPTER VIII - BIGGS GOES TO WORK

As Biggs is starting to work, Harry and Silvia are still in Houlton. They have decided to skip dinner with their new friend Moose and are planning the next leg of their trip to Presque Isle. Tomorrow they will pick up their car and drive the 40 some miles to their destination and temporary home. In the mean-time they have a leisurely dinner and watch two movies at the Inn.

"You know Silvia, I really liked *Murphy's Romance*. It was light and very entertaining. Sally Field was great. I have never paid much attention to the details and mechanics of acting but I was aware in this movie how Sally Field could get a message across with a facial expression, a twinkle in her big eyes or a variety of body movements. James Garner was, well, James Garner and the Carole King songs provided a natural background."

"I liked it as much as you did. By the way you use some of the same techniques to communicate that Sally Field did. You just don't know it. Or do you?"

"I haven't ever taken acting lessons, but since we left home I have started to learn a bit about that subject. I have a feeling that by the time we get home we both may be up for Academy Awards."

After breakfast the next morning, we get in the car and head north to Presque Isle. It's a short drive and takes us only about an hour. I am driving while Silvia has her Toshiba working to find out more about our destination.

"Harry, did you know that one of the attractions of this area is a scale model of the universe that stretches 40 miles from Houlton to Presque Isle?"

"No I didn't. Let me know when we are getting close. It must be spectacular."

"I will. I expect it won't be difficult to spot a planet."

It isn't very long before we pass the first planet in this model. It is nothing more than a Dunkin Donuts Munchkin mounted on a long pole. With all due respects to the people of the region, I am totally unimpressed by this model. And it doesn't get any better as we pass the rest of the Planets.

"If this is representative of the 40-mile-long

exhibit, I think it is plain silly."

"Harry. These models were built by High School students working under the supervision of the University of Maine at Presque Isle. Now we know that there is a branch of the state university in Presque Isle. Make a note of that because it may be a place for one or both of us to look for work. It says here that there are plans to expand the model into Canada."

"Somehow, I am still unimpressed but don't tell anyone. This model is clearly near and dear to the people here."

"I think that we should focus on Presque Isle itself in our search for a place to live. It is where the best possibilities for work are. We could probably live more cheaply in the more rural parts of the area, including Caribou and Fort Fairfield."

"I totally agree with that. We should take a few days to familiarize ourselves with the town before we try for any jobs. My first focus will be to look at the University and hope that I can find a job as a teacher's assistant or maybe even a low-level professor's assignment. My job at UNH may get me in but it's another state and who knows how they will view that?"

"My first choice for employment would be with the local police department so I could keep track of the criminal goings on and perhaps spot our Nazis if they start closing in on us. No way I would qualify for that, but maybe I could catch on with the newspaper, the *Star-Herald,* as a reporter covering the criminal goings on. That way I may be able to cultivate a few friends in the police department and/or the State Troopers."

After we have arrived and parked the car, I suggest to Silvia that we look for a place to stay for at the least the first night or two.

"I've already seen to that. There is the Northeastland Hotel right up the street. We can get a room there for $110 per night. Let's walk over there and see if we can book a room for a couple of nights. After that we must search for a less expensive place because we must conserve our dwindling cash supply."

"You think of everything. Now think of a way to get those Nazis off our backs. Personally, I'd like to see them dead and buried."

"I'll work on it. Don't hold your breath."

We approach the desk clerk and inquire about a room for two nights.

"Certainly sir. It's so early in the day that we have a wide assortment of rooms available. What are your needs?"

Silvia takes over. "We would like a room at the advertised $110 rate with twin beds."

"I can accommodate you with such a room at the $110 rate. Would you like to look at a room?"

"That's not necessary. Just book us in for two nights and we will go get our car and move it out in front."

"Might I see your credit card?"

"We will be paying with cash."

"That is a bit unusual in this day and age. If you pay the full amount in advance it will be fine. Will you need help with your luggage?"

"No, we won't but we will need to use one of your carts to bring the stuff in."

"That's fine. Go right ahead. The elevator is right around the corner over there," he says.

We cough up the $220 dollars and he gives us two keys to room 301. Actually, Silvia coughs up the money since keeping the stash is in her job description.

"I'll go get the car and be right back. The heavy lifting is in my job description."

I drive up to the front door and load everything onto the cart.

"What are you taking all of that stuff for?"

"Hey, I am not letting this typewriter out of my sight and I'm taking all the LL Bean clothes to cover it up in the closet."

The room is large and comfortable.

"I'd like to lie down and rest for the next couple of days," say I. "Maybe watch a dozen movies or so and have room service send our meals up here."

"Dream on loveman. Speaking of meals, why don't we get an early lunch somewhere nearby and then start walking."

"The Toshiba is getting a workout today. Let's see what you can find close by."

"The Café Sorpreso looks especially nice. Why don't we go there? It's an easy walk."

"It looks expensive. We'll go there but don't get used to it."

The head waiter meets us at the front of the restaurant with a smile. He has kind of a grim face and his smile appears to be very forced.

"Good morning, two for lunch?"

"Yes please."

It is very early for lunch so the place is nearly empty. So naturally he leads us to the worst table in the place. Just outside of the kitchen door in the far rear corner of the room.

"Excuse me, sir. We would rather have a table near the front."

"Certainly, sir." He utters this with a disgusted tone.

I decide not to tell him that "Sir" was my father, my name is Harry. It would be wasted. I order a Roast Beef Panino with Balsamic Garlic and Onion Jam, Swiss Cheese, Tomatoes, Red Onions and Spinach. Silvia orders a house salad and iced tea.

"Silvia, did you see the dinner menu? We have hit the mother lode. I can't wait to get back here for dinner."

"Plan on waiting a long-time buster. It's too expensive."

"Ok but we come back for dinner just as soon as we land jobs."

"Anyhow loveman, what is it about you that brings out the worst in waiters? Here we go again."

The waiter brings our food. It is delicious.

"The food is great and the place is elegant. Never in a million years would I have expected to find such a place way up here in potato country."

After a gooey ice cream dessert (Silvia takes a pass, as usual) we start our walking tour. The central business district of Presque Isle is mostly on the east side of The Presque Isle Stream, a narrow stream that runs north and south. There is only one bridge crossing the stream and this is on State Street. Obviously, the bridge makes State Street a principal downtown arterial. The major north-south street is good old Main Street. The Café, The Northeastland Hotel and other active businesses front on Main.

"Silvia, one of the things I want to do soon is look for another typewriter." I say this as we are walking past Hand Me Down Antiques, across from the Hotel. Further up Main Street is another shop called Buy, Sell, Trade.

"Dare I ask what you want with another typewriter?"

"Sure. I figure it would make our MDTW a bit harder to steal. A common thief would have to make off with two heavy machines or just pick one. If the latter happens we have a fifty-fifty chance that we lose the MDTW. If he takes both machines, I am out a few bucks for the second machine."

"You mean WE are out a few bucks. A few bucks we can't afford right now. In any event, it doesn't seem to me that it will keep the MDTW any safer."

"We'll talk about that later."

"Look at that. A real movie theatre undergoing renovation. Locally owned and one of a small chain."

We are now walking south on Main Street. We

pass Governor's Restaurant and Bakery. Further on a Dunkin' Donuts.

"We should get a bag of munchkins to take back to the hotel with us."

"We just had lunch for goodness sakes."

"Speaking of lunch, here's another place to eat. Governors' Bakery and Restaurant. There is certainly no shortage of places to eat here in town. I hope we'll have time to try them all."

"You could probably try them all in one day. If I let you."

"Aw, stop picking on me. You know you love me."

"I do but if you blow up to 400 pounds, I likely will stop loving the two of you."

I defer.

"Hey. Let's get a copy of the *Star Herald*."

By then we are back near the Hotel so we stop in there and get a copy. The paper is a weekly, published on Thursday.

"All that exercise has worn me down, Silvia. Why don't we go upstairs and rest for a couple of days?"

"You go ahead. I want to chat with the desk clerk for a minute. I'll see you in the room. Don't start anything without me."

"Funny."

I head for the elevator while she walks over

and waits for a gentleman to check in. I have no idea what she wants to talk about. After a few minutes the guest has checked in and Silvia moves in to talk. I take the elevator on up to the room as she begins to chat with the desk clerk.

"Hi. I'm Silvia Stein in room 301. I have a question for you. We have just arrived in town and love your hotel but it's going to take some time to find a place to live. I'm hoping you could recommend a less expensive place to stay while we look for a permanent place to live."

"Well, Mrs. Stein, I certainly understand. One Hundred and Eight dollars a night can rapidly add up to a small fortune. What I usually tell our guests is to look for a place over the border in Canada. It is a relatively short drive and if you don't mind you can find a less expensive motel room over there. Try the Maple Tourist Home, B & B. You should be able to book a room there for about $70 a night. Perhaps less if you reserve a room for a longer period. It is about 28 miles from here."

"Thank you so much. Would you happen to have their telephone number?"

"I certainly do. Good luck there even though we don't want you to leave."

"Many thanks."

She opens the door to our room and says, "I have the number of a place in Canada where we may be able to save about $40 a night. I will call them and inquire while you pick out a movie for us to watch tonight. Maybe two. Ok?"

"Sure, go ahead and call. I like this new role as social director."

"Don't get used to it because I retain veto power over the movie we'll watch."

"You mean we watch chick flicks?"

"Maybe one. Who knows what will strike my fancy?"

"How about The Playboy Channel? They have lots of chicks."

"You're a sick man."

"Maybe so but I expect to have this sickness until I die. And it's not what will kill me."

I search IMDB and find a movie that tempts me called *Cast a Giant Shadow*. It is based on a supposedly real story about the establishment of Israel and the events just thereafter. I am always dubious about Hollywood's attempts at writing history. I also don't care much for war pictures. I suppose this one attracts me because of my Jewish background. It also has an outstanding cast, including John Wayne, Frank Sinatra, Yul

Brenner, Kirk Douglas, Angie Dickenson and a woman I have never heard of named Senta Berger. She plays the female lead.

"We're in luck. I have made a reservation for a week at the B & B for only $70 a night and that includes breakfast."

"Sounds good to me. I don't know if I want to be constrained by having breakfast there every day but that's a minor detail and it is free. In the meantime, your social director has picked out a movie for us. It's called *Cast a Giant Shadow*. It's about the events leading up to the establishment of the Country of Israel, and the chaos that followed. Allegedly a true story about an American officer who returns to Israel after having fought in Europe and then returns to the USA. Eventually he unifies the disorganized Israeli forces and leads them into a successful campaign."

"Oh, lord! That is certainly not a chick flick but my interest is piqued. Put it on tonight's program. Maybe we'll find another one that is a bit lighter for a double feature. You ever wonder why there are no more double features at theatres?"

"I have indeed. Maybe the films are just too expensive. That wouldn't be cost effective when you can get the same revenue with only one film. Cost effective for everyone in the film industry but not for us moviegoers. I'm going to call the desk and see if we can get a pizza sent up. Is that alright with you?"

"Well. Um, Ok. Ask him for some out-of-town newspapers. Nice to keep up to date on the goings on in the country and the world."

"I will. Didn't think you would eat pizza again. We just had it recently. You sure you don't want me to search the town to find some tofu?"

"Good to break the rules every now and then."

"It is but you are in danger of becoming a serial rule-breaker."

There's a knock at the door. A young man has copies of the *New York Times*, the *Boston Globe*, and the *Wall Street Journal*. I tell him to put the papers on our bill and tip him generously for delivering them.

"Silvia, it's too early to have dinner. Would you like to try out the bed? It does look comfortable but you will never know unless you try it. If it's uncomfortable we might have to change rooms. If we wait too long they may be sold out."

"It's a deal that we get a chick flick after the war movie? You promise?"

"Of course. It's a bargain and I will hold up my end of it."

"You'd better."

That leads us to a very acrobatic encounter which proves satisfying to both of us. We snooze for a while afterwards, in that strange state that is neither asleep nor awake. I let Silvia sleep. When I call the pizza shop, they tell me it will be delivered in 30 minutes. While I'm waiting, I wander through the newspapers. The presidential election campaign is in full swing. It is strange to see both parties in such disarray. The Democrats are fighting to come together and push Hillary Clinton into the White House (and, of course, husband Bill) but they have many defections due to the treatment Bernie Sanders got and the mess of her damaging emails that continue to surface. The Republicans are also dealing with a huge fracture in the party. Many of the party leaders (and of course the press) are pounding away at Donald Trump. Hillary leads in the polls, with a couple of months to go. Unless she lands in jail it looks like she is a winner and Bill can have unfettered access to every one of the interns in the place. I have never seen a national political campaign like this one in my extensive lifetime. I hope I never see another one. According to the latest issue of the *Wall Street Journal*, Hillary and her vice-presidential candidate Tim Kaine have released their tax returns, a move called a diversion by Donald Trump, which it is, no doubt. Trump keeps burning bridges and his VP Candidate Mike Pence keeps trying to mend them. The latest polls suggest this is not working as the Dems have widened their lead to about 10 percent. We'll see. Meanwhile one of my favorite columnists, Peggy Noonan, has jumped off the election wagon for this week and writes about "the top is detaching from the bottom" all over the world. Whatever that means. Amidst all of this chaos, I am about to eat pizza and watch a war movie and a chick flick.

A knock on the door announces the arrival of the pizza. I kiss Silvia's forehead to waken her as gently as I know how. As I told you, I hate to wake anyone up, but especially her.

"Welcome back to the real world and our splendid dinner which will be served as soon as you put a cold, wet wash cloth over your forehead and wake up."

"Nice to be back. I can hardly wait to dig into this scrumptious, one-course extravaganza."

We eat the pizza and then watch *Cast a*

Giant Shadow. We both love it. All except for the ending which is the real ending and not a Hollywood one. I doze through most of the chick flick and don't even remember what it was. We are both sound asleep by 11 o'clock and don't wake up until the next day at 7.

CHAPTER IX - WE CROSS THE BORDER

After a quick breakfast at the hotel we check out, pack the car and head east for the Canadian border and the Maple Tourist Home B & B. It proves to be a circuitous route to the place. We drive north to Caribou on Route 1, then east on Route 89, north on Route 1A and finally east to the Hamlin/Grand Falls border crossing. It would have been immensely simpler to stay in the Perth Andover area which is directly east of Presque Isle but money is money and the prices are best at the place that we chose.

I stop the car a few miles from the crossing and say to Silvia, "You drive through the crossing and use your charm to get us safely through."

We switch places and she drives the final miles to the crossing and gets us in line. Silvia hands the border guard our phony licenses and passports while I hold my breath for what seems like 10 minutes.

"What is the purpose of your trip Mrs.

Stein?"

"Just pleasure. To be honest, we came here because we got a good rate at the Maple Tourist Home B & B."

"You have made a good choice. I know it well. My family stays there when they come here to visit. Have a pleasant stay."

"I'm sure we will and thank you so much."

Phew, I exhale and then direct Silvia to the Bed and Breakfast.

"Well, our credentials have passed their first test. Remind me to congratulate our favorite forger."

"Perhaps I should go on Facebook and let the whole world know about his skill."

"A few more of those not very funny lines and I shall be very sick."

"I plead guilty to the charge of producing lousy comedy. I trust the judge will go easy on me with the sentence. Maybe just a few months of public service."

"God help the public."

The B & B is located just west of the St. John River in Grand Falls, New Brunswick. The river makes a half circle there, producing a peninsular land area. The accommodations are terrific, as advertised. After we are checked into the B&B by our affable hosts, I get on the

Toshiba to find a map of the area and places to eat. First things first, no?

"You have made a great choice, Sylvia. We have hit the mother lode, you sweet, wonderful woman. There's a Burger King, a McDonald's, and a Pizza Boy right nearby, so plenty of good food here. All we need now is to find a Dunkin' Donuts to make it perfect. I understand that McDonald's is now serving lobster rolls. How about that for dinner?"

"You are joking, aren't you? There must be something else!"

"Well, there is some place named Le Grand Saut. Everything from shrimp cocktail to pizza. There are more eating places close by so we have options."

"Let's try Le Grand Saut, but before we decide, suppose we ask our hosts about it."

We do and they recommend it so we head there. I have Whiskey-Smoked Riblets and Sweet Potato Fries. Silvia chooses Scallops. The food is Grand.

"We need to have a battle plan for tomorrow and the next few days. I suggest that we stay here for 3-4 days. This will give us time to look for a reasonably priced place to stay back in Presque Isle, to familiarize ourselves with the place and look for jobs so we can preserve our cash."

"Sounds like a plan to me. Speaking of jobs, I'm going to try the University. Are you still aiming for the local newspaper?"

"I am. From a safety standpoint, I figure that is a good place for me to be. I would be able to keep track of the crime news there and it would be a good way to tap into the police. So, I'll try like hell to land a job there. I worry about my lack of credentials."

"Sure, but after all, you were editor-in-chief of your high school year book."

"Funny."

After lunch, we decide to drive back to Presque Isle to continue our walking tour, even though we'll only have a few hours before sundown.

"Let's both go to the University (UMPI) since I should be familiar with it even though I'm not going to do any teaching there."

The UMPI campus is located just south of the downtown area. We start at the admissions office and get a copy of the campus map showing all its facilities. It is a compact campus consisting of the usual attributes, including a lovely building housing the President. In addition, the campus has a daycare center, tennis courts and a soccer field. I guess this means this branch of the University does not have a football team. There's an auditorium and a gym/fitness center.

"Silvia, the place is a little short on athletics. No football, just soccer and basketball among the major sports."

"Oh boo. And here I thought I'd get a chance to show my skills as a quarterback."

"Sweetie, you are my quarterback. Just don't try an end-around play because I will flatten you in a second."

"Hah. Keep eating the way you do and you'll never be able to catch me. When did I become sweetie?"

"You've always been sweetie to me."

"You are becoming too adept at bull... Come on let's tour the entire campus."

We walk around and look at every building. We don't do any more than that because it is getting late.

"Harry. I have a good feeling about this place. I'm glad we decided to look it over this afternoon. Tomorrow I'll come back and talk to the head of the English Department about applying for a job."

"While you are doing that, I will continue my tour of the downtown and see if I can set up an interview with the *Star-Herald*."

"Let's have dinner here in town. Part of our familiarization process."

"I'm for that and I'll even pay for it."

"You'll pay for it? Have you come into some money that I don't know about?"

"Not exactly but I will reimburse you out of my first paycheck."

"You haven't even had a job interview yet."

"I recommend a first-class dinner at the Café Sorpreso. Soon, I will be bringing in the big bucks. More bucks then a typewriter shop can generate back home."

"You will? What the hell, we have had a productive day and I'm not in the mood for McDonald's lobster rolls tonight. Like I said not very long ago, just don't get used to this fine dining. You probably won't see it again for some time, if ever."

We drive back to the Sorpreso on Main Street. The maître de seats us at a good table where we can eat and watch the locals come and go.

"I'll have the Filet Mignon with Portobello Bacon Sauce."

"Can I get you a cocktail or something for a starter?" asks the waiter.

"I'll just have a large cranberry juice and shrimp cocktail."

"Very good choice, sir. And what can I get you, madam?"

"I'll have the baked haddock, but please ask the chef if he will leave off the dill crema and buttery crumbs."

"I'm sure that won't be a problem. Something to drink?"

"Just water, thank you."

We relax a few minutes in silence while we survey the other patrons and generally watch the comings and goings.

"You know I never would have guessed that you would find such a topnotch restaurant way up here in the northernmost reaches of Maine. When I think of Aroostook County I think of mashed potatoes, fried potatoes, French fries and potato farmers and not Baked Haddock with Dill Crema and Buttery Crumbs."

"I guess there are enough university professors and wealthy potato farmers to support this place. Certainly, your average worker here will probably never see the inside of Café Sorpreso."

"Nope, not at these prices."

When the waiter returns with our meals I ask him what he knows about the history of the Café.

"I only know that it was opened in 2007, so

it's only about nine years old. I believe that one of the chefs came from England but I'm not sure about that. The staff here believes it is the finest restaurant in all of Aroostook County and maybe in northern New England."

"We would agree with that and we do have a lot of experience everywhere along the east coast."

"The food and the ambiance are terrific," Silvia adds.

We eat our meals at a leisurely pace, savoring every bite. I think the food and the ambiance have blocked out from our minds the reason we are up here in the very north of New England. This is a good thing, so I eat slowly, adopting Silvia's normal pace. It takes us several hours to finish our meals, pay the check and leave the Café. During that time, there is a turnover of diners and they appear to be brothers and sisters of the group that was here when we arrived. We leave the Café about 9 o'clock and stop at the Northeastland Hotel to see if we can get some recent issues of the *Star Herald*. It is close to ten o'clock.

"Do you mind if I catch the end of the Patriots pre-season game?"

"Go right ahead but use the headphones so I can read."

It is surprising that I can get the game in Canada. The NFL and its teams rake in billions of bucks every year. Money talks and billions shout. The NFL has been scheduling games in England for a few years. If I remember correctly, they are playing one in Mexico this year. This appears to be pointing in the direction of expansion outside the USA. I love football even though my high school only played soccer. On the other hand, my college, The University of Miami, has a bigtime football program. The Patriots are playing the Chicago Bears without their all-time great quarterback, Tom Brady. Brady is serving a four game suspension at the beginning of the regular season and will not make an appearance. Jimmy Garoppolo, his backup, plays a very good game as does the third string quarterback Jacoby Brissett. The Pats win the game. That makes them 2 and 0 in the preseason. It is north of eleven o'clock when the game ends. Silvia has long since gone to sleep and I drop into the never-never land minutes after my head touches the pillow. Force of habit gets me up early. Five A.M. early. I shower and shave and by that time Silvia has just started to stir. I let her climb into consciousness without my help. I hate to wake anyone up but especially her.

"Good Morning, love of my life. Nice to see you."

"Good morning yourself. How long have you been up?"

"About an hour or so. How are you feeling?"

"Well, not raring to go yet but I will be after a long hot shower. Did your beloved Patriots slice up the big bad Bears?"

"Not exactly. It was only an exhibition game and I don't think any of the players go flat out, because no one wants to risk a serious injury in a preseason game. That's just me talking. As you know, I never played a minute of football in the NFL."

"Nor anywhere else."

"You mock me. The Pats did win. Not by much but a win is a win and they looked rather good at times during the game."

"I'm happy for them and for you, macho man. Let me at that shower."

"While you are in there I will go through the recent issues of the *Star Herald* to find out what's going on in the area."

When she finishes her shower, and is dressed, we decide to have breakfast here at the B & B because it comes with the room. Our cash is starting to shrink to an alarmingly low level. We meet and chat with several of the other guests at the Inn. Maybe I'm a snob, but none of them are particularly interesting.

Back in the room, I sit Silvia down and say, "I'm going to take a few minutes before we leave for PI and tell you what I read in the local paper. It's another way to familiarize ourselves with the area. We both need a lot of that and quickly. We shouldn't appear to be as dumb as we are about the place when we start interviewing for jobs."

"Start talking. You have my full attention."

"First, the crime news. You will be pleased to know that a vicious killer from Florida came up here and killed another man. They were both in their 80's. The killer took a bus back to Clearwater but he managed to get himself on a Walmart Security tape. Witnesses also claimed to have seen both men together. The harvesting of the area's vegetables started in earnest around the first of August and officials claim that 16% of the folks who live in the State have something called 'Food Insecurity.' I guess that means they are hungry or in danger of being hungry."

"And the good news is what?"

"Well, the judge denied bail for the Florida killer."

"Is that the best you can do?"

"Hey, I don't make the news, I just report it. The town of Easton has filed suit against the County Commissioners alleging they are giving undeserved tax breaks to six Amish farmers. Oh yeah, the Maine DEA busted a meth lab in Washburn that was operating about 1,000 feet from a school.

"And, a PI man was arrested after he wouldn't leave the Walmart Store. He was holding up a sign that had the cent sign on it."

"Are you ever going to get to the good news? Or is there any?"

"Oh sure. Residents of the area are now able to take a law enforcement course without travelling out of town. Sounds like they need a lot of graduates from this course. Finally, the railroads in the area are making improvements to their tracks, which handle a large amount of freight. That's just a few of the articles from the August 3rd and August 10th issues."

"Sounds to me like this place is just like anyplace, USA, riddled with crime. I wonder if the residents are happy with all this crime."

"When I get on the *Star Herald*'s staff, I will do a man in the street survey. That should be good for two lead articles. To answer your question, the people are not happy with all this crime. PI is the 'Epicenter of Anxiety,' so says a story from the August 17th issue. They are quoting a New York Times story which is based on the number of times that people Google the word 'Anxiety.' Maine is the leading State and PI is the leading metropolitan in the state. "Interesting someone in New York is calling PI a metropolitan area? The author talks about economic levels, the low level of education, and opiate withdrawal as causes of this anxiety. An official of the Acadia Hospital in Bangor says there aren't enough mental health providers up here. He adds that the residents should use online sources as an alternative."

"Goodness. Let's get out of town right now!"

"Somehow, I believe that most of this is overstated, if not totally wrong. On the other hand, the August 17th issue carries stories of at least 11 local area residents involved in drug trafficking, including heroin. That's the bad news. The good news is that they all have been indicted. There is a story about the death of a Mars Hill woman who crashed her car into a house. But what the heck, that's not in PI and it could and does happen all the time in all kinds of places."

"Oh, right. I'll start packing the bags again."

"No. No. Wait. There is more good news. The

local Ruby Tuesday restaurant will not be one of several in the state to close and a new community center is set to open soon."

"I guess we are staying, huh?"

"To coin a phrase, The Die is Cast."

"Try coining a phrase with more pleasant words. I am too young to die."

"There are some classified ads that are of direct interest to us. I see ads for three different apartment complexes. They're the Town and Country, The Scovil, and Williams. The Williams looks good to me. We will start there in the morning. Ok?"

"Sure."

"The Williams has two-bedroom apartments starting at $550 per month. Add them to our morning agenda. The sooner we find a place the better. Maybe this morning. Yes?"

"Aye, Aye boss. But you better drive today. After hearing about all the anxiety, I am much too full of it to drive to the town."

I am steady at the wheel all the way back to PI. No anxiety here. When we arrive, we drive by all the apartment complexes and decide to try The Williams first. As we sit in their parking lot Silvia looks at me and asks, "How do we respond if their application for an apartment asks for references and other information which we can't supply?"

"First things first. We'll find the agent and ask to look at whatever vacant apartments are available. If they have something that suits us we will figure out a way to supply the information. Maybe we can get someone to use as a source or maybe convince the agent that he or she really doesn't need it. Sometimes the sight of cash makes things happen, or in this case go away."

A stylish looking woman is staffing the office. Dressed smartly in a dark business suit that contrasts and focusses her blonde hair. A nameplate on her desk says <u>Marcelle Williams.</u>

"Hi, Ms. Williams, my name is Harry Stein and this is my wife Silvia."

"Good morning. Nice to meet you. Have a seat."

"Thanks."

"What can I do for you?"

The woman appears to be highly organized judging by her physical appearance and that of the office. She is cordial but maintains a business-like veneer.

"I must say it is nice to be dealing with the owner."

"Actually, my husband Jack is the owner."

"Close enough. We have just arrived in PI

and are looking for an apartment to rent. It must be furnished because we are not sure how long we will be here. We'd rather not ship our furniture, until our plans firm up."

"Well if you want something on a month to month basis, I'm think we can accommodate you."

"Well, we are willing to sign up for a 6-month period and pay the entire amount up front."

"If you are willing to pay 6 months in advance, we will certainly have something for you. How many rooms do you require?"

"We'd like at least two bedrooms, one of which we would use as an office."

"There are some details we can talk about, but first let me show you what is now available. Once you have a look we can come back and go over our lease requirements. Come with me."

We can tell she is in charge by her words, which fall just short of an order. Husband or no husband we are talking to the boss. We follow her out the door.

"One of the vacant units is over there close to the street, and the other one is over there beyond the pool."

"Let's look at the one closest to the street first."

"Sure, come with me."

We follow her to the apartment which is not far from the office.

"It is right here on the ground floor with parking for two cars very close to the front door."

"Do you have any units with a garage?"

"No, we don't. The front door opens into an entry way. There is access to the two bedrooms off to the left and the kitchen and living room off to the right as you can see. The apartment is furnished only with the basic things but we can modify that to suit your needs if what you want is available on our site. The rental price for this unit is $550 dollars per month. That includes all utilities."

"I think I like this one and it would be ok to be close to the street. We are used to traffic noise. I'd rather hear that then a bunch of noisy kids trying to drown one another."

The apartment is freshly painted but sparsely furnished. I catch Silvia's eye and she gives me a barely perceptible nod.

"This one will do. Can we sign a lease now and how long will it take for you to get it ready?"

"Depending on your needs it will only take us a few days to have it ready. You certainly can sign a lease now. C'mon back to the office and we will get the paperwork done."

We follow her back to her office. She hands us a standard lease. Well, I think it's standard but then again, I have never leased an apartment.

"The only thing we'd like to have would be a desk in the second bedroom. Is that a problem?"

"Hold on a minute and I will find out."

She dials the phone.

"Hi Pete. Do we have any desks in the warehouse or in a vacant apartment? I have a nice couple who are about to lease apartment 77 and they need one. Thanks Pete.

"You are in luck, there is one in a vacant apartment that we can bring over this afternoon. How will you be paying the rent?"

"Well, we have just arrived, as I said, and don't even have a local checking account yet. I can pay in cash if that works for you."

"Works perfectly."

"Great. I assume that we will be responsible for linens and things, but anything else required of us?"

"Nothing. The rent includes all the utilities and the apartment comes with two parking spaces. We can have the apartment ready for you as early as the day after tomorrow. Is that soon enough?"

"It's fine. We are staying at a B & B in Grand Falls. The day after tomorrow is good."

"Well then, thank you and welcome to Presque Isle. I hope your stay is pleasant. If there is anything else that you need, come see me. We always try to accommodate our tenants. Here are two keys to the apartment."

"Thanks, and have a great day."

As we leave the complex, I turn to Silvia and say, "This is our lucky day. I certainly didn't anticipate finding an apartment so quickly and easily. The housing God is smiling on us. A good day to buy a Powerball Ticket."

"We just spent over $3,000. And why the hell did you go and offer to pay for six months up front? I don't suppose that the size of her boobs had anything to do with it. That was plain stupid. We can't afford a ticket or anything else for that matter."

"Aw. Don't be a Gloomy Gus. Do you want to stop by the University and talk to them about a job? Are you familiar enough with the town to do that now?"

"My knees get a bit wobbly when I think about that. Besides I am really, really pissed at you. I could use another few days of getting acclimated to the area. Shoot, I'll bite the bullet and at least find out how the process works.

Give me a few minutes to simmer down and then we can go."

At the University Silvia picks up an employment application at Preble Hall, the Admissions and Administration Office. She tells the Administration person that she will take the form home, fill it out there and come back tomorrow and submit it.

"How come you did that?"

"Did what?"

"Took the application with you instead of filling it out then and there?"

"Fear, I suppose. My background is so weak in terms of academics that I need some time to figure out how I might shape it to give me some chance of getting on board."

"My advice to you would be to come clean and let them know upfront that your background is weak but you know English, know how to teach and how to write. I think you can handle all that very nicely. You must have some confidence in yourself. If you don't, it will be easy to read. Your UNH teaching experience should qualify you if they have an opening."

"Easier to handle a job flipping burgers at Burger King. There's no guarantee that New Hampshire experience will count for much up here."

"Hey. This is a side of you that I don't see often. I suggest that you look at this in terms of survival. We both need decent jobs to make it through this ordeal. Where is the Silvia that I used to know?"

"Aw shucks. I'm still here somewhere. I just need a day to pull myself together. Survival is important to me, I'm too young to die. Unless we just give up and sell the MDTW to the Nazis."

"I think we have talked about that alternative. It's my thought that that would literally be a dead end. The Nazis will not likely leave loose ends around. And that's exactly what we would be, two loose ends. Besides that, it would be a cheaper course of action for them. They wouldn't have to pay us for the MDTW. Think of this as survival."

"You are right, of course and I don't like to think of myself as a loose end. Or any kind of an end, for that matter. It's time to find you a job. Ready to try the newspaper? I promise the old Silvia will surface tomorrow morning. Maybe even this afternoon."

We take the car over to the offices of the *Star-Herald* at 40 North Street, which is right downtown. After we find a parking space, I tell

Silvia that I want to talk to them alone.

"Hah; who's the big baby with cold feet now?"

"Guilty. Why don't you shop for a new fur coat while I embarrass myself privately?"

"I'll do that. Could I have your credit card please? I'll see if there is a Frederick's of Hollywood here in town".

"There you go, the old original Silvia is returning. The wise-ass Silvia. The hilarious Silvia. Leave now!"

She leaves. I enter the office and ask to speak to Steve Frederick, the editor.

"Mr. Frederick is in a meeting just now with one of our reporters. If you could wait a few minutes, I think he will be free to talk to you. May I tell him the nature of your visit?"

"Yes. I hope to find work on your reporting staff. My name is Harry Stein and I only recently arrived in PI."

"Have a seat Mr. Stein."

"Mister Stein was my father. I am just Harry."

"Ok, Harry. Make yourself comfortable. You will find some old newspapers on the table in the corner."

"Ten minutes later she goes into the editor's office and comes out with him in tow."

"You must be Mr. Frederick. Harry Stein."

I extend my hand which he shakes vigorously.

"Mr. Frederick was my father. I am Steve."

He glances at his secretary while she tries to hide a giggle without much success.

"Come on into my office so we can talk. Have a seat. What brings you here today?"

"My wife Silvia and I have just arrived in PI and are looking for work. She is hoping to work at UMPI. I was hoping to land a reporting job on your newspaper."

"My goodness. What a coincidence. The guy who just left my office was one of our best reporters. This must be a message from the newspaper God because I don't believe in coincidences. Is there any particular area of reporting that interests you? Do you have any writing experience?"

"While I will work hard in any reporting role, I have a strong interest in writing about crime and its impact on the community. And no I don't have any experience on a newspaper. Outside of being the editor of my high school yearbook about a hundred years ago and writing copy for my typewriter shop in New Hampshire, I have no writing experience. I am a quick learner though."

"Our full-time reporting staff is quite small,

as you might expect. This means we are much like the Patriots and each player must be very versatile. Interesting. I didn't know there were shops that specialized in typewriters, anymore."

"There aren't very many. A handful scattered around the country."

"I'm afraid you won't find any of them around this office."

"I didn't expect I would but I am also good on my Toshiba."

"If I could find a place for you, how soon could you start? I have a gap I need to plug as soon as possible. I think what I need to do is give you a chance to write a piece for the paper. I certainly like your spunk."

"I couldn't possibly start until tomorrow morning."

"This would be a test and if you passed it, I will put you on the staff. Assume that there is a murder here in town involving a man who has suddenly taken a pistol and shot his wife and his best friend. Take it from there and give me a piece that would be suitable for the front page, above the fold."

"Thank you. See you in the morning."

"Aren't you even going to ask what your salary would be?"

"No. Let me have a two-week tryout and we can talk salary after that. Ok?"

"Alright. You are one unusual guy."

"That's what my wife says, only the word she uses most often is weird. See you tomorrow morning."

"Bye."

I call Silvia on her cell to ask her where she is.

"I'm at the mall. No fur coats and no Fredericks of Hollywood. Sorry. But I did manage to find a smart new ensemble that I can wear when I have a job interview at UMPI".

"Too bad about the Fredericks. Can you pick me up?"

"I am just standing at the cash register. Are you finished already? "

"I am."

"Why don't you walk up to that antique shop on Main Street and I'll meet you there?"

"OK. That's Hand Me Down Antiques. Right? See you there."

I get there before Silvia and start looking around. Surprise, I see a portable typewriter. When the owner spots me looking at it he approaches and asks, "Are you interested in typewriters?"

"Hi. I am interested in certain kinds. What I'm looking for is a large office machine. Preferably an Underwood model. Do you have anything like that?"

"Not here but I might have at home. I have a large barn with stock stored in it. I could look tonight. Are you going to be here overnight or are you just passing through?"

"My wife and I have just moved here. Speak of the devil, here she is."

"We could stop in tomorrow morning if that would give you time to search your barn. What time do you open in the morning?"

"I am generally here at about ten.

"I am starting a new job tomorrow morning so I won't be by until lunchtime."

Later, in the car, Silvia says, "Wait until you see what I bought at the mall."

"And you wait to hear the news I have for you."

"We can go home tomorrow?"

"No. But the editor of the paper has given me an article to write and if I produce a good piece, I'm hired."

Silvia drives and we are back at the Inn in a half an hour or so. As soon as we get to our room she starts to unpack her bundles and undress at the same time.

"Yum, this is a terrific surprise," I say as I too start taking off my clothes.

"Not now you sex fiend. I just want to show you what I bought."

She grabs one of the packages and heads for the bathroom. Disappointment for me.

"You look great," I say when she comes out of the bathroom.

"Thank you. If clothes make the man they can make the woman as well. Now, see what I have for you. You need to look spiffy if you expect to do a good job at the newspaper."

"What do you mean if? I already have the job as a reporter provided I pass the editor's test. He didn't seem to care a wit about my clothes."

"You're kidding me. Right?"

"Of course, I'm not. In fact, I expect to spend this evening writing away like mad."

"I'll be dammed. When do you have to hand in your test article?"

"Tomorrow morning at 8 o'clock."

"Really. I thought we might have a date."

"We can. I will only be spending a couple of hours or so on the feature. "

"What's it going to be about?"

"Well it's a hypothetical story about a man who picks up a pistol and shoots his wife and best friend. I take it from there."

"That seems like an old and oft repeated theme. Do you have a hook in mind? By the way may I enquire about your salary?"

"Not sure yet."

"Are you serious?"

"Absolutely. It was my idea to have a two-week tryout and then talk dollars. Have faith."

"Sometimes I don't believe you. Sometimes I do believe you and that can be worse yet.

"If you don't get it done in two hours, I may go looking for a pistol. Why don't you just write the whole thing right now?"

"I will but first you have to ply me with wine and a luscious dinner. If I can be honest with you, I am jealous of you because you have beaten me to the ranks of the employed."

"Don't be. I'm positive you will land a job. And soon."

"I'll check the Toshiba for restaurant advice. Here we go, Le Grand Saut, right here in beautiful Grand Falls. Get your best duds on, I am taking you to dinner."

"If you think that would speed up your production of your test article, by all means let's go quickly."

We drive to Le Grand Saut, which is not very far, and enter what looks to be a very quaint restaurant both inside and out.

"Very cool," says Silvia, once we are seated.

"My thought exactly. What is your pleasure?" I ask, after the waiter has dropped off our menus.

"Nice going Harry. You got nary a scowl from the waiter. I will write home about this. And then ply me with fine wine and I will tell you what my pleasure is. If I'm sober after dinner, I may show you my pleasure."

"I love it when you talk dirty."

"Don't get ahead of yourself. I haven't suggested anything dirty yet."

"Well, I have pictures in my head."

"You always have dirty pictures in your one-track head."

"You must admit I am on the right track."

Just then, the waiter arrives and saves me from sticking my foot any further into my mouth.

"Can I get you folks something to drink?"

"Of course, you can. I'll have a carafe of your best burgundy wine and my husband will have a plain seltzer because he is the designated driver."

"Are you ready to order dinner or do you need more time?"

"I'm ready."

"You are always ready to eat. Designated

drivers wait for their passenger to order and I am not ready."

The waiter departs with a shrug like he's seen this before.

"I intend to get one-quarter sloshed my good man, so don't rush me."

"Yes boss. Have you noticed that a substantial number of the diners here are speaking French?"

"And that must make it difficult for you to eavesdrop. No?"

"Oui."

"Here are your drinks," the waiter offers when he returns.

"I notice that some of your patrons are speaking French. Is this unusual?"

"Not at all. About 22 percent of Canadians speak French. Most are in Quebec but there is a sizable French-speaking minority here in New Brunswick. Many of the French-speaking people also speak English."

"Thank you for that information."

"And are you ready to order dinner now?"

"Yes. We are," says the boss. "I will have a Shrimp Cocktail and Atlantic Sea Scallops with Roasted Red Peppers."

"A good choice, madam. And you sir?"

"I'll have Whiskey Smoked Riblets and a side

of Sweet Potato Fries. Would you make the Riblets rare, please?"

"Of course. May I get you more wine, Madam?"

"Yes, you may cuz I don't have to drive."

When he returns with another carafe of wine I look at Silvia.

"You really are going to get sloshed, aren't you?"

"You are damned right and not one half sloshed but COMPLETELY sloshed. You may have to carry me to the car."

"My pleasure, madam."

"When I hear the word madam, I think of a woman with a house full of women. In other words, a brothel."

"There you go again talking dirty."

"Our meals arrive and I am not surprised that the food is excellent."

After eating we return to the B & B and fall into bed. Just sleep for Silvia while I slave away on my homework for Frederick.

CHAPTER X - SCORE ONE FOR SILVIA

I drive to PI and drop Silvia off at UMPI first thing in the morning. It has taken a bit of prodding on my part but she finally agreed to drop off the job application and press for an early interview.

"Good luck, sweet. Just remember, you will make a terrific professor and make them believe that."

"I'm just going to drop off the application and set up an interview."

"Sure. Just make them want to interview you before someone else snaps you up. There are other places to teach around here and they know that."

"I know but the others are smaller and are less attractive to me."

"I understand that's true, but they don't know that. So, don't show them that. And make sure you don't let them know that you are here for a short time."

"C'mon Harry. How dumb do you think I am. Besides, if I do get an instructor's appointment maybe we'll decide to stay here forever."

"Now you're kidding. Right?"

"Sure I am."

She opens the car door and says she will call me on my cell when she is finished so I can come pick her up. I drive to the *Star Herald* intending to check in with Steve Frederick. Fredrick's door is closed but I can see through the window that he is busy with another staffer. When he's done with the other staffer, he beckons me into his office.

"Let me take a look at your test article."

He speed-reads through the article in minutes. I suppose a newspaper editor needs to develop this technique. Maybe I can learn to do this. Watching him, I am nervous. I hope it doesn't show.

"Looks good to me. You still interested in the job?"

"Yes sir, I certainly am."

"Good. My name is Steve. Sir was my father. Let's talk salary. As a beginning cub reporter, I can only offer you $400 a week with no overtime and you must be ready to go out in the field to follow a story right up until press time. I'm sorry I can't offer you more but it would upset the balance on the rest of the staff. Still interested?"

"Yeah, Steve, I am."

"Good. You are hired as of this minute. First thing you do is to introduce yourself to the staffers who are present. Then come on back and we can go over your assignments for the next issue."

I wander around and introduce myself to everyone who is in the office. Joshua Archer is a most active staff reporter. His stories cover the entire front page of a recent issue. Christopher Bouchard is also active with a front-page article on County Tourism. Both have photographs along with their stories. I make a mental note to see whether my old Nikon is up to the task. I hope so because our money situation is tight enough so that I don't want to invest in anything new.

There are several articles in a recent issue with the byline BDN. When I go looking for BDN, I am told it stands for *Bangor Daily News*. I wonder what that is all about. Then I find out. The *Bangor Daily News* is the parent company of the *Star-Herald*. I check the stories and see that they do feature news from outside the PI area. Places like Houlton. I make a mental note of this since we are loosely connected there with Moose. I see that Frederick is now alone in his office so I rap on the door."

"C'mon in. What's happening?

"I saw that you were busy so I spent some time outlining some routine stories on criminal activity including the Troop F report. I also wandered around and introduced myself to everyone who is working just now. I have given some thought to a feature article. Let me run it by you."

"Shoot."

"I thought a man-in-the-street type story might be interesting. I go out and interview a sample of residents in PI and get their views on crime in the area. Are they interested in reading about criminal goings-on here? Are they aware of the scope of these activities? Are they happy with the level of enforcement? Is there anything they think needs changing? Do they follow crime and corruption outside PI? In the State? In New England? In the rest of the country? In foreign countries?"

"I like it. Start on it immediately. I'll put it in the next edition on the front page. This means it must be ready in two days to meet the deadline. Concentrate on that and I will shift the other stuff to the rest of the staff. I like the way you have hit the ground running."

"Ok. Let me out of here. I will start on it

now."

"Good. Anything you need, let me know. Get some pictures of anyone who doesn't mind seeing their mug on the front page, but don't pressure anyone. Sometimes people will be straight forward with a reporter so long as they are not identified. I imagine this would especially be the case when they are talking about the police department."

Before I leave the paper, I grab a clipboard, lined paper tablets and a few pens. The office staff fixes me up with a press badge. I decide not to call Sylvia, just in case she is in the middle of something at UMPI. Instead, I drive over there and find her. She has a happy look on her face as she approaches the car.

"Thanks for stopping by. I have great news. I managed to wrangle an interview before the committee on the day after tomorrow. I was told that one of their English professors is leaving shortly for a better job on the main Campus in Orono. They are anxious to fill his spot. There's not much time before the fall semester starts. I think the chances are pretty good that I will land a spot on the faculty."

"That's great. I have good news as well. Frederick liked my test story. Hired me on the spot. He also likes my idea for a man-in-the-street story and has scheduled it for the front page of the very next issue. I have my work cut out for me but I will make it one way or the other."

"May I offer any help you may need? In the not too distant future, I expect to be an Assistant Professor of English. I can help you in setting up the questions and who knows what else? Did you finally get around to salary or are you going to wait until the end of the year for that?"

"More sarcasm. He could only offer me $400 a week without upsetting the balance in the office. Your help is gladly accepted and indeed needed. After all I am just a dumb-assed reporter with all of 4 hours of experience. I have all kinds of trouble with the English language and I can't spell worth a damn."

"And what do I get as payment for this help? After all, university professors don't come cheap."

"I know you are kidding but there is one thing I can promise you. When you are making up your lecture schedule for the fall, stick me in it. I will come and tell your students all they need to know about crime and reporting on same."

"I like that. You're on."

"I tell you what. Why don't we pick out a good spot somewhere on Main Street where we will conduct the interviews? And then we can make up a list of appropriate questions to ask. That would be better than trying to do that at the Inn."

"Good idea."

"How about right near the Café Sorpreso?"

"You mean so we can eat afterwards? Will you ever be able to get food off your mind?"

"No. Not as long as I'm alive."

"I figured."

"We find a parking spot near the Northeastland Hotel on Main Street where the sidewalk is wide enough for us to set up a small card table."

"This looks like a good spot to set up camp, don't you think?"

"We are at what you would call the 100% corner. Suits me. It's time for the English Professor to go to work and whip up the proper wording for our questions."

"When did these become OUR questions, Loveman?"

"I believe in using talent where you find it and you are IT."

I prepare a list of questions with the help of my in-house talent. After about an hour we have the routine pretty much worked out. We have a quick lunch at a forgettable restaurant after which we drive back to the B & B. I go over the routine one more time, clean it up and write out a readable copy. The survey must be done in two days to meet the paper's deadline. It's convenient that Silvia is available to help.

"What do you say we have dinner at Le Grande Saut and then watch a movie back here? Bed at 11:00. An early start on the street in the morning, say about eight. That way we may be able to catch some men, er, I mean people on their way to work."

"You just remembered that women work too. Huh?"

"You bet, and I will make sure that women are well represented in our sample. You know how I love women, right?"

"Right, especially blonde ones with large chests."

We have another great meal at Le Grande Saut and then watch a movie entitled *Brooklyn*. Some people would call this one a "Chick Flick" and I would agree. It's a light romance set partially in Ireland and partially in Brooklyn with an Italian love interest thrown in. It is not a heavy drama. We have an early breakfast at the B & B. For the first time, we meet an interesting couple, named James and Sally Smith. My antennae go up when I hear a couple named Smith talking with a decidedly heavy Germanic accent. I cast a quick glance at Silvia. I read her eyes. She is having the same reaction that I am. When we leave the B & B we discuss our sense of the two people.

"I wonder if we are both developing severe cases of paranoia," I offer. "When a troop of heavy duty bad guys have chased you all the way into the northern most region of the country, a bit of paranoia might be a good thing. But is probably just a coincidence and we are making a mountain out of a mole hill."

"Maybe so, but I am going to stick their names and faces in the corner of my underdeveloped brain for future reference."

"Me too. By the way woman, we need to call the B & B sometime today and tell them we are checking out so they can have a bill ready for us in the morning."

"Let me do that. I have some rapport with our hosts and I'd like to leave on a high note. I may try to wheedle whatever information they might have on the couple supposedly named Smith."

"You go girl. If there was ever a good

wheedler, it's you."

First thing in the morning we drive straight to "our spot" near the Northeastland Hotel. I set up a small folding table and tape a small sign to the edge of it. It reads "Star Herald Newspaper."

With my ID badge firmly attached to my shirt, I begin approaching pedestrians, one at a time. For the most part they are agreeable and speak freely at the beginning. There are some who pull back and change their mind when I tell them I want to talk to them about the Police Department. Several of them nearly turn and run away. Maybe I exaggerate but it would be interesting to know if they are hiding something. Like for example a long criminal record.

"Did you notice the few people who turned and have left when I tell them the subject matter of the interview?"

"I did. Makes you wonder. Maybe there is some way you can follow up with another feature story about them."

"Maybe there is. I'll think about an approach when we have wrapped this one up."

"Well, look who is walking up the street toward us."

I turn in the direction she is facing and there

are our old friends, the Smiths.

"Hello there. I never expected to see you two here in PI. I'm doing man-in-the-street interviews for a feature story. If you live in PI or plan to live here, I can interview you."

"No. I'm sorry but we do not live here and will not be settling here either."

Too bad. I'd really like to interview the hell out of them individually and compare their stories.

"Good luck with your survey," says Jim Supposedly Smith as they saunter off and out of sight around the corner on State Street.

We look at each other without a word and I continue the interviews. After a good four hours, we have collected enough for a good story.

"I am going to skip lunch and go back to the office and write the article. What are you going to do in the meantime?"

"The 8th, 9th and 10th wonders of the world. My husband is going to skip a meal. I was hoping to come along with you and perhaps help you do some editing with the article."

"I never say no to an offer of help. Particularly one that comes from a beautiful woman. Let's go."

"You are so suave. I can't stand it."

"No, I really mean it, lovewoman."

The two of us drive over to the *Star Herald*. I introduce Silvia as an English Professor at UMPI to the staff that is there. We go over the interviews, select the ones that are good and compose the story. It is done in two hours. I leave it in the editor's box and we depart for the B & B.

"When we get back to the B & B you need to do two things."

"Good that you know what I need to do."

"Hey. You are a much more talented soul then I am, so like I said before, never let talent go to waste."

"And what is it I should do?"

"First, let our host know that we are checking out in the morning so she can have our bill ready. After thanking her for a lovely stay, see what you can learn about the so-called Smiths."

"Oh yes, oh master. And have you written a script for me?"

"Come on Silvia. This is serious stuff and anything we can learn may save our lives in the future."

"I know dumbbell. A little humor can go a long way in reducing the stress on us, so grin and bear it."

"Look, the Smith's car is not in the parking lot so they are not back yet. Go do your thing."

Silvia goes into the office while I go to our room and start to pack our meagre belongings. The MDTW is still hidden in the closet under the pile of LL Beans clothes. This reminds me that I promised to check the antique shop to see if he has located another machine for us.

In a few minutes, Silvia comes in with her news.

"Our friends the Smiths have checked out. They gave an address in Houlton as their home. We should be able to check with Moose to see if that is phony which I kinda know it is. What do you think this is all about?"

"There could be many reasons why they are here and probably using a false home address. Because of our circumstances, my first supposition would be that the Nazis are on our trail and they were sent to keep an eye on us. On the other hand, they may simply be shacking up and the false address could be a way of preventing anyone like a husband or wife to track them."

"What in the world can we do about that?"

"Not much but we can be alert and be ready to run on a moment's notice. I doubt that they would try anything in public so we should avoid being alone by ourselves. We could possibly go to the police or even hire a bodyguard. Since we really don't know for sure that the Smiths were here to keep an eye on us we should wait a bit before we do anything drastic. If we went to the police, they would probably laugh us out the door. Nice job of wheedling the information out of the B & B owner though."

"Por nada. I also paid our bill by the way. We can stay for breakfast in the morning or not, as we wish."

"Are you up for one last meal at Le Grande Saut?"

"Sure. Let's go for an early dinner. I need to be fresh in the morning for my interview and a long night's sleep will help."

We do dinner and return to the B & B. Silvia hits the sack immediately and starts making soft snoring noises after about 10 minutes. I start to think what I might do for a follow up story to the street interviews. I decide that logically I should get a reaction from the police department on what the people are saying about crime. Good. I'll work on that in the morning. My paranoia moves me to push a chair against the door before I go to bed. Too many bad movies and TV shows.

In the morning, we do have breakfast at the

B & B (it's included in the room rent and a penny saved is a penny earned). I load up the car and we head for The Williams Apartments. We already have a key to the place. When we enter the apartment, we are pleasantly surprised. They have done a great job.

"Look. They even found a desk for the second bedroom and the paint has been freshened up here and there. While you are having your interview at UMPI, I will pick up some linens and towels. Is there anything else we will need?"

"Well, soap, shampoo and TP. Forget about groceries, I don't trust you with that. I'll do that later."

"OK. I'm sure you will knock them dead. Good luck."

"Bad choice of words, especially for a writer, but thanks for the sentiment anyhow. Keep your cell on. I'll call when I am done."

She knows my feelings about cellphones. I hate them and frequently leave mine turned off. There are some modern conveniences that I would just as soon be without. A cellphone tops the list. We cart our stuff into the apartment and I drop Silvia off at the university.

The first thing that I do when I get back to

the apartment is to call Moose with my throwaway cell. I didn't want to do that from the newspaper office for reasons of confidentiality. The Sears operator puts me on hold while she connects me to the automotive department and tracks down Moose.

"Good morning Moose. This Harry Stein. How are you today?"

"I'm good. And You?"

"I'm ok. The reason I am calling is I wonder if with all your contacts, you might be able to find out some background facts on a couple of people up here."

"I can try. Are they bad guys?"

"Well, I'm not sure. Silvia and I have been staying at The Maple Tourist Home in Grand Falls, New Brunswick for the last few days. A couple showed up at the Inn and then they also turned up in Presque Isle where we were doing some work. Maybe just a coincidence and maybe they were tracking us. They are registered under James and Sally Smith and they spoke with a heavy Germanic accent. They also signed in as residents of Houlton. I thought that you might be able to check around and tell us whether there is such a couple in the Houlton area."

"I will check all my sources here but I'm very

sure that there is no such couple by that name living around here. I'll make some calls and get in touch with you tonight."

"Great. Call me on my cell. The number is 878-6401."

"My regards to Silvia."

I remember that I might have a typewriter waiting for me at the antique shop so I stop there. The owner has dug a large office typewriter out of his barn. It is not the same model as the MDTW but it is a large office model of a similar vintage and will suit the purpose.

"I kind of like that large office machine if it's not too expensive."

"Excellent, the price is only six hundred dollars."

"Um, that is out of my price range," I offer. I have slipped into my negotiating mode. "Sorry," and I start to move toward the door. I can see him flinch a bit and I know I have him hooked.

"You seem to know your typewriters. What would you pay for it?"

"If it were in pristine condition, I would pay six hundred dollars for it. Obviously, you can see that it is extremely dirty from sitting in your barn and rust has started to develop in the interior which will be very difficult and time consuming to get rid of. With that in mind. I would pay $250.00 for it. It's so full of rust and dirt I may never be able to make it work."

"Alright, you have a deal."

I plunk down three one hundred-dollar bills, get my change and head for the apartment where I stow the machine away in a closet. Next up is the Aroostook Centre Mall. I roam around and pick up some bed clothes, towels and other odds and ends that we need. Also, some cleaning materials that I will need to put the new typewriter in better condition. It's now close to lunch time. Just a few minutes before noon, my cell chirps.

"You may come pick me up. I'll be waiting for you in front of the Campus Center Building."

"See you in a few minutes."

She is waiting for me on the sidewalk and I know by the smirk on her face that she has good news.

"Am I looking at college instructor Stein?"

"No, you are not."

"Oh, by the look on your face I thought you had some good news."

"I do. You are looking at UMPI's newest Assistant Professor of English. Please show the proper respect."

"I bow down to you and will be your love slave for 24 hours. However, since you are now gainfully employed, dinner will be on you. By the way, I picked up some bed clothes, towels and some of the other necessities for our apartment. We can try out the bed, just as soon as you make it."

"You caught me at the just the right moment. I might just buy you dinner and put you to work as my love slave. But first we need to stock up on groceries. I noticed a market named Graves Supermarket right on Main Street. We'll go there for the basics and then try and find a health food store."

"Your love slave is here to help."

It takes us about an hour and a half to load up on the basic foods and condiments. Silvia reads just about every label in her search for all natural ingredients. It takes her twice as long to grocery shop than anyone I know. Back at the apartment we put the food away.

"I've looked on the Toshiba trying to find a natural health food store but I don't see one that works for me. Let's postpone that for another day and make dinner now."

"Bummer. I was looking forward to some tofu. I'll just grin and bear it."

"I'm sure you will grin, at least."

By now you probably have guessed what she makes for dinner. A gigantic salad made with mostly organic veggies and two tiny hamburgers. I am thankful for the hamburger even though it is barely four bites. I fill up on lettuce, carrots and cucumbers. Better than nothing.

"What's for dessert?"

Great, she was not able to find any So Frozen Almond Milk. I can't stand almond flavored anything. And wonder of wonders, she settled on Haagen-Dazs ice cream. I am an ice cream snob and refuse to eat most brands but Haagen-Dazs is at the top of my list. I spruce up the plain vanilla with a liberal dollop of blueberry preserves.

After dinner, we outfit the bathroom with towels, washcloths, soap and the other personal essentials.

"Help me make the bed, Harry."

"Gladly."

"Don't get your hopes up too high. We've had a long and tiring day. All I have in mind is sleep."

Moments after I fall asleep, the phone wakes me.

"If this is someone's idea of a joke, it ain't

funny." I almost turn the phone off but then I remember Moose promising to call.

"Harry, don't hang up. It's Moose."

"Sorry, Moose. I forgot you were going to call. Silvia and I both had tiring days and fell asleep a few minutes ago."

"Oh. I'm sorry. I can call back tomorrow morning."

"No, go ahead. What did you find out?"

"Plenty. I checked the area like I promised and there are a lot of Smiths in the area but none living in or around Houlton named Smith who speaks with a German accent. So, my feeling about them was correct. Given that I suspect they are up to no good, I would avoid them like the plague."

"The damage has already been done. They haven't done anything illegal as far as I know so I can't go to the police. We will just watch out for them. My sense is that they are simply keeping track of us and mean us no immediate harm."

"Ok. But if they are following you they must be up to nothing good. Do you want some protection? I know people up there."

"Thanks for asking. We appreciate your concern and we may ask for some more help later."

"Are you armed?"

"Well, no. Can you help with that?"

"Yes. I know of several shops in and around PI."

"I'd rather not buy any guns here in Presque Isle. If they are following us, I'd rather they thought we were unarmed and helpless. You follow my reasoning?"

"Yes, I do. How about in Caribou?"

"That'd be great."

"Try Big Al's Gun Shop. It's a small shop in an out-of-the-way location. Don't be put off by its run-down appearance. They do good work and their prices are reasonable. They can also train you in the use of the equipment they sell. Tell Al that I sent you."

"Thanks Moose. You might tell your Uncle Steven up in New Sweden to be on the lookout for us, just in case we need to get away from here in a hurry."

"I will. His number is 207 492 8885."

I hang up and hear Silvia mumbling, "Who was that?"

I think that's what she said.

"Nothing. Later. In the morning."

At breakfast, Silvia remembers the call and asks again who it was.

"That was Moose. He called to tell us that

there was no one living in the Houlton area who fits the description of our friends the Smiths. No surprise there. Moose was concerned that we were walking around with bad guys tracking us and that we were completely unarmed. Unable to defend ourselves, if it came to that."

"What are you holding back? I read you like a book and I know there is more."

"I was going to wait until after breakfast to tell you when you are less likely to get upset. Moose thinks we should arm ourselves and it makes perfect sense to me. He has a friend up in Caribou who has a gun shop and firing range. We'll change our plans for today drive up there and buy a couple of handguns."

"What do you mean? A couple of hand guns. How many does one man need?"

"Only one but you should have one as well."

"WHY ME? I've never touched a gun in my life. I'm scared to death of guns."

"Exactly our point. Better to be scared of a gun than to be dead by one. Now's an appropriate time to touch one and to learn how to use it. Don't you think? Your life might depend on it. Ok?"

"Ugh. I think I'm going to lose breakfast."

"Which is why I wanted to wait to tell you."

"Ok. I will grit my teeth and do it. But why are we going all the way to Caribou?"

"I didn't want our friends to know that we were armed, so I was the one to suggest a more remote place where it would be difficult for anyone to follow us. As long as we drive around before we leave and make sure that no one is following us we should be able to get to Caribou without anyone knowing. We need every edge we can find and if the bad guys do catch up with us we will need them to be close enough before we whip out our guns and blow holes in them. Can you be ready in 15 minutes?"

"Sure. This danger has been hanging over us like a dark cloud but now it feels like it's not a cloud at all but a heavy lead weight on top of my head."

"We shall overcome; we shall overcome."

"Lord. Your humor sucks," she says. But I detect her struggling to hold back a giggle.

"Ok Annie let's go get your gun." This does draw out a full laugh or two from her, albeit with a bit of a nervous edge to them.

We get in the car and drive slowly around downtown PI to make sure that no one is following us. No one is, so I head north on Route 1 toward Caribou. When I get out of town, I call Big Al and tell him we are on our way. Moose has already talked to him and he tells me that he has several hand-guns in mind and will spend all the time we need to learn how to handle them. Then, we can practice on his range for as long as we want. I tell Silvia the details of our conversation as we drive. I detect a small sigh from her which she tries to cover up. Good, I think. She is getting used to the idea of having a gun in her purse.

"I notice that you keep looking back out the rear window. You don't see anyone following us, do you?"

I know she doesn't because I have been watching in the rear-view mirror.

"No. There was a bright yellow SUV behind us for a few miles it turned off onto a side road."

We arrive at Big Al's without incident. Big Al is big. I mean bigger than Moose. I'd say six and a half feet tall and pushing 300 pounds. His place is deep into the woods on a narrow dirt road that needs some grading. But it is passable. Guy that big doesn't need a gun to protect himself. We enter his shop which is shabby looking on the outside. It's so bad that I worry that Moose has sent us to a third world gun shop. The inside is quite another story with enormous displays of rifles, shotguns and hand guns. All the major manufacturers are in the house.

"Hi. My name is Harry Stein and this is my wife Silvia."

"Hello. I'm big Al the owner of the best gun shop east of the Mississippi. I got a call earlier from my friend Moose down in Houlton. He said you were in some kinda trouble and needed to arm yourself. Have you owned firearms in the past?"

"Well I used to have a BB gun and I have fired a 22-caliber pistol owned by my friend Murray Burnstine. That was ages ago so you could say I really don't have any experience."

He smiles and says, "I think we should start at the beginning. Does your situation call for a rifle or shotgun? Or are you looking for small handguns to carry on your person?"

"Our situation is such that we want to be armed all the time with small concealed handguns. I know that severely limits our range but that's ok since the bad guys following us won't expect us to be armed."

"OK, then. What I would suggest to you is that you both buy a small handgun that you could easily conceal. That means you would need the bad guys to close in to about 10 feet before you pull it out and fire if they don't stop.

A gun that you hide in a pocket or in a purse will have limited accuracy, by definition. So that is about your only choice. Are you each going to be armed or just you Harry?"

I glance out of the corner of my eye at Silvia. I can see immediately that she is disturbed at this unintended sexist question. She draws in a lung full of air, stifles the urge to snap back at him with sarcasm and simply says, "I want to be armed as well. This is the reason I am here. You should understand that the guys chasing us are ruthless and would kill a 6-year old child to get what they want. To say nothing of an adult female."

"Now I begin to get the seriousness of your situation. You'll forgive me if I didn't grasp that from Moose's telephone conversation. Now that I understand, you both should buy identical weapons for several reasons. You may need to be able to use the other's gun. Since it is identical to your own there will be no wasted learning time in terms of the both the operation and maintenance of your gun. In addition, you will be using the same ammunition. Make sense to you?"

"That sounds very sensible to us, Al. Do you have a specific make and model in mind?"

Am I kidding? Of course, he does.

"Yes. I do."

As he is talking, he walks over to a display case filled with many different makes and models of handguns and takes out one without hesitation.

"This is a Remington model RM380. It has a barrel length of just under 3 inches and an overall length of just over 5 inches. Its height is less than 4 inches. You can see it will be easy to hide in a pocket or a purse. It is light weight and has a trigger pull of 10 pounds. That's enough to prevent accidental discharge but well within your average adult's capability to fire in a smooth fashion without jerking from the kick back. It has a 6-shot magazine."

"I like the feel of this gun. Incidentally, I was born and brought up in a small Connecticut town near Hartford. I remember that Remington had a manufacturing plant there. Do they still make guns there?"

"Remington is the oldest American maker of firearms, dating back to 1816. It has a new plant facility in Alabama and other facilities around the country. Corporate headquarters is in North Carolina. The principal manufacturing plant for guns is in Ilion, New York. Other than knowing this gun was made in the USA, I can't be more specific."

"I notice you have several other makes of hand guns. How do they compare with Remington?"

"They all are of good quality or they wouldn't be here in my shop. Having said that, if it were me I'd pick a Remington over all the others because they are less expensive or more expensive."

"We trust your judgement on that. How expensive are they?"

"Well, they list for $436 each. When you add in taxes and ammunition you'd be up to a bit over $1,000."

"Arming ourselves properly is important to us as we have said but that's a lot more than we hoped to spend. Are there any less expensive alternatives?"

"Sure. I can cut the cost about in half by substituting rebuilt ones."

"That sounds good. Just where are the guns rebuilt?"

"Right here in my back room. If any parts are needed I use factory-made replacements. I even have a fully equipped machine shop where I can and do customize all manner of firearms for my customers."

"Terrific. We have a deal."

Al gets out two model RM380's out of the

back room along with cleaning and oiling kits and instruction manuals.

"Let's sit down over at that table so I can show you all about the RM380."

We sit there with Al for about 20 minutes while he explains how the guns work and how they should be cleaned and stored.

"It's a good idea to go over the guns periodically even if they haven't been fired in a while. Now it's time to for a real-time bit of practice firing so out to the range we go."

We go outside to the range where Al demonstrates good shooting essentials to us.

"First, as you first begin to get used to the gun, I would encourage you to use a two-handed grip. You will get better accuracy using two hands. When you get more proficient I want you to try a one-handed grip because there are situations that can develop where a one-handed grip will be better. It will be a tad faster as well."

Al shows us both one-handed and two-handed grips, how to squeeze the trigger so as not to disturb the aiming and how to anticipate the recoil. Then he posts three targets about ten feet from us and hands us our guns. Silvia asks him if she can use ear protection when she starts shooting.

"Yes and no," says he. "At first you can, but after a while I want you to take them off and fire some rounds without them. After all, you won't have them on if someone attacks you, so you need to experience the noise and be ready for it so it doesn't distract your aim. These targets are 18 inches in diameter which represents the average body width below the shoulder. Always aim for the center. As you get more proficient we will use smaller targets. OK. I'm going to fire a few rounds and then you guys do the same."

He fires 5 rounds and all of them hit the target very close to the center. I follow and I hit the target twice out of the same 5 tries but the two hits are out near the edge, on each side.

"That's pretty good for openers."

He points out the mistakes I made and signals for Silvia to take a turn. She does and misses the target with all five shots.

"Don't worry about that. Just keep practicing and you will be fine."

Then he shows her what she did wrong and then starts to walk back to the shop.

"Hey, where are you going?"

"Inside to do some bookkeeping. You guys keep firing 6 shots at a time, each. When you are not shooting stand back and don't even load your magazine until the other one is finished and backed out of the way. You can stay as long as you want and only pay for the ammunition you use."

We practice for an hour and a half and both of us improve dramatically. We are worn out after this session and ready to head back to PI. Back inside, Al looks over the targets we used and seems pleased with the results.

"You both did well. Better than I would expect for people who have never fired a gun before. I would recommend at least one more practice session and maybe two more. Come back when you have some time but make it sooner rather than later. Good luck and thanks for your business. I'm not buttering you up. I mean it. Take care of yourselves and if there is anything else I can do for you, let me know".

"Thanks Al. I'm sure we will be back soon."

CHAPTER XIII –
ENTER MARCOS AND HIS BALLOON

With tha,t we get in the car and head south to PI.

"You know what might ensure our safety in the immediate future would be to hide the MDTW in some secure place away from our own apartment. The Nazis are after it and it is reasonable to assume that they won't harm us so long as they don't know where it is. Then again, we would become a loose end when they would, no doubt, find it."

We drive the rest of the way in silence. Each of us struggling to see an easy way out of our situation that won't involve shooting our guns.

"If those guys were standing in front of me right now, I would shoot them without a second thought."

"That could well be illegal. It's also a silly idea. You need grounds for killing anyone, including guys you know are evil. What we need to do just now is to find Graves Supermarket and stock up on food for our pantry."

"That's what we need? When in doubt eat. Right? Sounds like me talking, sweet stuff."

"Until something better comes along. Yes."

"Hey. Something better has come along. It's called sex."

"Lord. Are you ever going to grow up and stop acting like a teenager?"

"Hope not. Last time I looked, teenagers must eat too. Head the car to 797 Main Street."

We get to the supermarket and park in their lot. My guts are telling me to go lightly because I see us leaving town soon. Maybe that's just wishful thinking. Perhaps it's just more paranoia. We shop for an hour or so, and spend about $150 and buy enough food for about a week.

"You stow the grub while I take a quick check around the parking lot."

"Stow the grub? You grow more like a gunslinger with each passing hour."

Back in the apartment, I say, "With all this food we just bought, I don't guess you wouldn't want to eat out. Huh?"

"You guess right. Go in the living room and read the *Star Herald* or some other profound written work while I whip you up some proteins."

"Don't forget the carbohydrates and skip the

tofu."

I need to get back to my job and it would be best to go back with another feature story ready to go in the next issue. Something other than one on crime to demonstrate my versatility. I struggle to grab hold of something that might work. Ordinary business or crime stories? Nah. Politics? Nah. Got to be something fun and light with a new approach. Sports? Too routine. It pops into my head in a flash of light. The town is host to a balloon fest every year. That would be it. I'll go up in one of them and write it while I'm in the air. Maybe take a video and stick it on You Tube or Facebook. Great idea. And great fun to boot. I go back to the kitchen for Silvia's input on my idea.

"I thought I kicked you out of the kitchen once tonight. Are you going to keep disobeying the commander's orders?"

"Be serious for a moment., I need to see what you think about my idea for a feature story. There is a balloon fest here in PI. There will be twelve pilots from around the globe participating. All I need to do is convince one of them to let me ride with them. I'll take photos and a video which we can also put on Facebook."

"Are you talking about one of those hot air balloons that actually go up in the sky without brakes or steering wheels?"

"Not exactly. They claim to be able to steer the balloons somehow, and to stop it, they can always drop to the ground."

"Fabulous. Drop to the ground. You can't be serious. You just can't be. Try something else."

"I am very serious and it will make a great story. Remember, I have a press card and shouldn't have any trouble convincing one of the pilots that it would be great publicity for him to carry me up on a flight."

"Be even more publicity if he crashed with you in the balloon. Maybe knock off a few people on the ground."

"I think I detect a touch of sarcasm in your voice. Maybe not. Anyhow, tomorrow morning I'm going out there and get me a pilot."

That evening we step back in time a bit and watch the movie *The Sting* with Redford and Newman. We'd both seen this one before but still enjoyed it one more time. After a breakfast of Heritage Flakes cereal with strawberries and apples, I give Silvia a peck on the cheek as I leave to find a balloon pilot who will be overjoyed at having a newspaper reporter along on his next ride. She is cool and dismissive, letting me know that she is still against this idea.

Using my reporting and sleuthing skills I quickly find out where Marcos Bonimcontro from San Paulo, Brazil is staying while in town. Marcos captains the *Tribirds* balloon. I'm in luck because he is eating breakfast at the hotel. The desk clerk directs me to him in the dining room. I'm hoping he speaks English as I march in and introduce myself.

"Good morning Mr. Bonimcontro. My name is Harry Stein of the Star Herald newspaper and I wanted to speak to you sometime today, when you have a moment."

"Now is a good time. Why don't you join me for breakfast?"

Great. He speaks English better than I do.

"Thanks. I've already had breakfast but a cup of coffee would be nice." Don't tell Silvia, think I, caffeine is on my no-no list. Marcos summons the waiter, who brings me a steaming cup of rich dark coffee. Even if I don't get a story out of this escapade, the coffee will make my day.

"Mr. Stein, what can I do for you?"

"I'd like to write a front-page story for the paper about the balloon fest. But I'd like to take a different approach and go up for a ride and write the story up there. I'd take photographs of the balloon and yourself on the ground before we go up and then take photos, make notes and perhaps take a video in the air. In addition to the story, I'd put the video and the rest of the package on Facebook or Twitter. How does that sound to you?"

"Of course. It sounds wonderful so long as you say positive things."

"I can't imagine that I could find anything negative to say even if I wanted to, which I don't."

As we talk, an antenna goes up in my brain. I can't help but wonder if Marcos has any connection or information about the Nazis who are hunting us. Probably just more paranoia on my part, but I stick that question into an empty corner of that brain. I will think of a way to see if Marcos knows anything at all about the Nazis. First things first though.

"When do you think, we could go up? I will need just a bit of time to clear the idea with my editor and gather the equipment I will need."

"I prefer that we do this either before or after our regular flights. This afternoon would be ideal if that gives you enough time to get ready."

"That works for me. Is the weather ok for

you?"

"Sunny and warm with very little wind. That's perfect. I'll meet you at the site at 2 pm."

"I hate to show my ignorance, but where is the site?"

"It is on Spragueville Road, not far from the Aroostook State Park."

"See you there."

I drive back to the apartment to pick up my cameras and to have lunch.

"Hey, lovewoman, I have just had a great talk with Marcos Bonimcontro, captain of the good ship *Tribirds*. And we are setting sail at two o'clock."

"While you have been gone, I have done a little research on this festival. Guess what? Last year in Texas, eighteen people were killed in a crash. Did your Mr. Bonimcontro happen to tell you about that fiasco?"

"Umm, no he didn't. But Silvia, bad things happen in all sorts of everyday situations and events. You know something like 35,000 people die every year in auto collisions. We don't let that stop us from driving. Thousands more die in accidents in their homes. You can't stop living because there is danger in the world."

"Does that mean you have to go looking for dangerous activities?"

"But that's just the point: riding in a hot air balloon is not any more dangerous than riding in your car on Interstate 95. Or climbing up your stairs."

"I admire your courage but I still think you should dream up another story. I never heard of 18 people getting killed all at the same time on a staircase."

"I'm too far into this and besides I think it will be a prize winner."

"If it's ok with you I will stay here and not go out to watch it."

"Ok. What are we having for lunch?"

"Anything you want to make for yourself."

Obviously, she is punishing me for going against her wishes. Seems awfully childish to me but I know her heart is in the right place and she is only concerned with my safety. I start pulling out the makings of a cold chicken sandwich but before I get very far into it, Silvia relents.

"Never mind with that sandwich. If you are going to crash and burn I'll see that it is with a full stomach. A rare steak and mashed potatoes coming up in 15 minutes."

I give her a big hug and start gathering the things I will need: a couple of pens, the ubiquitous notebook, my Nikon camera for stills, and the video camera. After lunch, I thank her for being a sport and I head for the *Star Herald*.

When I tell Steve Frederick about my idea, he seems to like it but I see some hesitation on his part.

"What is it Steve?"

"Well, I should really run this by our legal counsel. I'm a bit worried that our accident insurance might not cover this activity. When are you planning to go up?"

"This afternoon about 2 o'clock. Don't worry about it. I will sign any release you want so that the paper is not liable for anything that may occur."

"Ok. I'll get one typed up in a few minutes. Do you have everything that you need by way of equipment?"

"Now that you ask, I suppose a small voice recorder would make it a lot easier for me rather than the old notebook and pen."

"That's easy. I'll get you one that can be used in the voice actuated mode. I don't know if it will work in that mode in the balloon with all the background noise but you can try it. If it doesn't work, you can still use it in a non-actuated mode. Anything else?"

"Nothing comes to mind except some drugs

to calm me down."

"I can't help you there. See your local pharmacist. Come by after you are back on the ground so I can see what you have."

"I will and thanks."

I arrive at the launch site a few minutes before two o'clock and unload all my equipment before Marcos arrives. His crew has already unpacked the balloon and started the propane heaters which will fill up the balloon with hot air to get it off the ground. When he arrives, he greets the crew and walks over to me with a smile on his face.

"We have nearly ideal weather conditions with only a little wind. It's enough to carry us over the town so you can get a good view from up there. We will probable try and stay at an altitude of about 1,000 feet. Climb on board and let's take off."

I feel a bit queasy despite of all my pronouncements to the contrary.

Now I know how an astronaut feels. Well, sort of. The wind carries us down over the downtown area. I can see The Williams Apartment Complex and I imagine I can see Silvia through the roof of our apartment. I have cranked up the video camera and taken a bunch of stills with the Nikon. The voice actuated recorder works fine and I make verbal notes while operating the cameras.

We drift over the downtown and to a large open area on the edge of town.

"Look down there. You can see our crew with the chase vehicle following us to the landing site. They will make it there before we do. I am going to turn down the heaters so we can land. Sometimes the actual touchdown can be a little rough so hang on tight."

Is he kidding? I am holding on so tight I worry that I will tear the basket apart. We bump down hard and the ground crew grabs the tether lines and it's over. I made it. I let out a large amount of air from my lungs, much like the balloon did.

"Marcos. Before you leave, I will probably want to talk to you again and maybe get you to read the story before it's published. Would that be OK with you?"

"Yes, it would and I will be around town for another week, so ring me up anytime."

Next thing I do is whip out my cell and call Silvia.

"We're down sweet wonderful woman. We just landed without incident and it was just great. I got reams of notes on my recorder and a ton of still and video pictures. What are you up to?"

"Nothing. I am curled up in bed with the blanket over my head but otherwise everything is normal. Come on home. I might have a surprise for you."

"Keep the blankie over your head for a while. I'm going back to the office and write up this prize-winning story while it's still fresh in my mind."

It is nearly five o'clock before I finish going over my notes and selecting the photos I want to use. It is a full-length story. Frederick is delighted with it. By that time almost the entire staff has left for the day. He quickly scans the written story and goes through the still photos that I have selected.

"I like it. I love it. It will have great appeal to our readers. Do you have the video?"

"Yes. Right here."

I have boiled down the video to about 10 minutes. He loves that too.

"Let's get that on Facebook and Twitter right away."

I do that and then pack it in and head for the apartment. Silvia greets me at the door with a giant hug and a few small kisses.

"Woman. I am taking you out to dinner tonight to celebrate writing this story. It's your choice of restaurants."

"Does this mean that you are buying?"

"No, course not. But that's not important. Just put away your apron and let's go. I feel great."

"The Sorpreso?"

"Naturally."

I won't bore you with a long-winded commentary on our meal at the Sorpreso. It's enough to say that we enjoyed another elegant meal. It measured up to any dining experience we ever had.

"You know, Silvia, I think I could get used to living up here if I was promised one dinner per week at the Sorpreso."

"It's a grand place but maybe not reason enough to move here."

"A small exaggeration, I suppose."

We arrive back at the apartment just in time to watch the New England Patriots play their first regular game of the season. Despite playing with an injury-ridden line-up and without Tom Brady, who is serving his suspension, they beat the Arizona Cardinals on their home field. Jimmy Garoppolo, Brady's back,-up plays a great game. It doesn't end until close to midnight so we slip under the covers. No fooling around tonight.

"Don't forget that we have a lecture at UMPI tomorrow," says Silvia.

"I did forget. Remind me what it's about".

"The importance of the news media in maintaining a free society. We will try to span the full range of the media."

"Nothing that hasn't been done before."

"I know but don't forget that we will be talking to a bunch of youngsters who spend far more time at athletic events than they do worrying about their freedom. We all tend to take our freedom for granted."

"Until we wake up one morning and find that we have delegated the definition of that freedom to a nameless bureaucracy. Or we find out the hard way that we haven't been paying enough attention to a foreign dictatorship. Remind me what time this great event takes place."

"Sarcasm is my job. Remember?"

"Sorry for the intrusion into your territory."

"I am going to spend the morning here in the apartment working up a detailed outline for the lecture. And you?"

"I'm going over to the paper and gather some routine crime stuff for the next issue. I'm also going to track down my favorite balloon pilot and see what I can find out about the Nazis in his home country and his relationship to them, if any."

"You don't really believe there is any connection. Do you?"

"No, I don't. This balloon fest was scheduled last year, long before our ordeal began. Nevertheless, I'd like to know where his sympathies lie. It is not beyond the realm of imagination that the Nazis could have enlisted him into their hunt for us."

"I'm sure it's just more paranoia on your part but it's certainly worth and hour or so to talk to him. PROVIDED YOU DON'T TALK IN HIS BALLOON!"

"No way. I've had my fair share of balloon riding."

When I drive over to Marcos' motel, I find him relaxing at the pool.

"Hi, Marcos. I don't want to bother you but I do have a few more questions for you. They have nothing to do with balloons but just something I'm interested in finding out about your home country."

"No bother at all. I don't spend much time there because I am on the road all the time. I'd be glad to help if I can."

"I'd like to develop a feel for the kind of society that Brazil is. My interest stems from a desire to visit there sometime in the future (a lie). We all know that your country was home to a large contingent of Nazis who escaped Germany after World War II. Are they still there? Are they an important element in the society?"

"I would tell you that I know that there is a core of Germanic people who are undoubtedly descendants of those original bad guys. I believe they are not very active in public affairs and pretty much hang out with their own kind. They are there. There is not much we do about that. They command a significant slice of wealth and as far as I know are not involved in criminal activity in any major way. Said another way, the people tend to tolerate them. Are there any warm and fuzzy relationships with the locals? Probably, but again they are not obvious to the average guy in the street."

"Marcos, it is kind of you to be so frank about that subject. I want to thank you. I suspect that I will not be visiting anytime soon. If I do get there I will try and find you and take you out to dinner."

"That would be great. Here's my business card. But I would be the host and dinner would be on me."

I leave Marcos, satisfied that he has no

knowledge about the Nazis who are chasing us. Back at the newspaper I prepare some routine materials on the current crime scene.

There is the usual report from the State Police Troop F. At the Aroostook County-Superior Court, in Caribou, we see some minor probation violations, operating after, a minor assault, trafficking in drugs, and a life in prison sentence for a man convicted of murder. I hope this is not so routine. The fire marshal in Masardis has charged two men with arson. I make a note to find out where the heck Masardis is located. There is a report of a three-vehicle crash on Parson Street that sends three people to the hospital. A report of a woman being extradited from Oklahoma.

The Presque Isle Criminal Docket for the month includes the following items:

Burglary
Refusing to submit
Illegal possession
Criminal mischief
Speeding and numerous DUI cases
Numerous unauthorized taking cases
Disorderly conduct
Terrorizing
Trespassing

Domestic violation
Littering
Illegal possession of a fish
Allowing a dog to be at large

It's clear to me that I need to do some research on the nature of many of these crimes. Everything from allowing a dog to be at large to murder. I will try to keep this edition away from Silvia. It would make her even more nervous about staying here.

Back at the apartment Silvia is busily making an outline and notes for this afternoon's lecture.

"How did it go with you?"

"Number one, our friend Marcos has absolutely nothing to do with the bad guys in Buenos Aires. He even invited us to dinner should we visit down there. Heaven forbid."

"That's one less thing to worry about. And did you prepare some crime stuff for the next issue?"

"Yeah, sure, a long list from several different sources."

"Anything interesting?"

Since there is no fooling her, I decide to come clean.

"There was a wide variety of crimes ranging

from allowing a dog to be at-large to murder. Lots of driving under, speeding, burglary and others. Some of them I don't even have a clue what is involved. Oh yeah, there was a three-vehicle collision right here on Parson Street. Three people to the hospital but the good news is with no life-threatening injuries."

"Oh. If there is no more good news, I think I will crawl into bed and pull the covers over my head. Wake me up when it's safe to go home."

"Your attempt at levity falls flat. I know you'd tell me if you saw our friends the Smiths around, but have you?"

"No certainly have not. Don't worry I would scream bloody murder if I did. So, go over this afternoon's lecture with me."

We spend about 30 minutes going over her outline for the lecture. It consists primarily of a brief introductory lecture on the importance of a free press and then questions from the students and answers from us. That assumes the kids are interested enough to ask some questions. If they don't, we will have some of our own ready.

We have a convenient lunch of frozen Pad Thai, which tends to be Silvia's fall back choice when time is short or she's just plain lazy. It's also happens to be the only way she can get tofu into me.

Silvia's class has about 50 students. I am surprised that they seem to be paying rapt attention to her. I don't know if that's because she is smart and beautiful or maybe she has a great delivery. They even ask relevant questions. Lord. After it's over, some of them gather around Silvia and pepper her with more questions. I am totally ignored so I slink back outside and wait for her at the car. We find ourselves without much of anything to do that evening. Silvia cooks a real meal (no tofu). The steak and home fries are delicious. She even eats some herself. Wonders never cease.

"Tomorrow morning, I think we should drive up to Big Al's and practice some more on his range. And since we are almost halfway there I want to drive on to New Sweden and get acquainted Moose's uncle Steven Gustafson."

"Why do you want to do that? Is there something you know and are keeping from me?"

"No. It's just that I keep feeling the bad guys getting close to us and I want to be prepared for a quick getaway. Call it a premonition or just more paranoia. A feeling I can't shake."

"If you want to invest the time to do that tomorrow, I'm with you."

"If you have things to do, I can go by myself."

"Not on your life."

"Then since that is tomorrow's plan, lets watch a movie and get some sleep. Oh, and by the way, you did a great job with the kids today. They ready liked your lecture and Q & A afterwards.Very impressive."

"After all, I had expert help. Did I not?"

"Not. They didn't even know I was in the room."

"Sure, they did. But I suspect they know who will be grading their exams."

"I never thought of that."

"But, I was terrific. Wasn't I?"

"Truly you were and still are. Therefore, you get to choose a chick flick for tonight's feature presentation as a reward."

"Let's see what Meryl Streep movies Netflix is offering. Why don't we watch *Kramer Vs Kramer* with Dustin Hoffman? Haven't seen that in a while. And it's not really a chick flick so you can stay awake and watch."

"Ok. I'm with you."

The movie is a good one, but still it's hard for me to watch a movie when it is still in my mind from the last time I saw it. I try to appear attentive and I think I fooled Silvia into thinking that I really enjoyed it. This was another one of those nights when we both were only interested in a quick hug and kiss before we fell asleep. We ought to be well rested for tomorrow, that will be a very long one. After breakfast, we drive around PI long enough to make sure we are not followed and then head straight north toward Caribou.

"I think we should start out with some shooting practice first and then work our way up to New Sweden to meet with Moose's uncle Steven, as we talked about last night. You know it's still not too late to change your mind. We can still turn around and head back to PI."

"And leave me here alone? Are you crazy? Besides I need practice shooting much more then you do. Drive!"

We shoot (pardon the pun) up Route 1 to Caribou and arrive at Big Al's a few minutes before he opens. He seems genuinely glad to see us when he finally opens the door.

"Good morning you two. You here to buy a machine gun or did you just stop by to say hello?"

"Good morning to you too. Correct, we were just in the neighborhood and stopped to say hello."

"However, since we are here, we'll do some shooting on the range."

"Great. Same deal as before. Use it all day if you want and pay only for the ammo that you use. After about 50 rounds I'll be out to see the results."

"Deal."

After a few rounds, I can see the improvement in the accuracy for both of us. After the full fifty rounds, I tap on the door and Big Al comes out and examines the targets.

"Excellent. Both of you are getting very good. I feel sorry for the bad guys if they ever catch up to you."

"I know that shooting at a stationery paper target is a lot easier than trying to plug a live human being moving at you. Still, I do feel more confident than I did before we started. Practice may not make perfect in this case but I have made progress and Silvia has made even more."

We fire a few more rounds with Big Al watching.

"Enough is enough. Your arms must be getting tired because I can see it in the results. So, get out of here. I hope to see you again. And if there is anything at all that I can do to help, just holler."

"You're right. My arm is getting tired. See you again and thank you for the offer of help.

You never know."

As we head up Route 161 toward New Sweden, Silvia calls Gustafson on her cell while I listen to one side of the conversation.

"Is this Steve Gustafson?...Sorry to bother you so early in the morning. My name is Silvia Stein. My husband Harry and I would like to chat with you."

"Yes. I know that Moose has talked with you. We are in Caribou and since we are not far away, we thought we'd like to come up now. Good. Can you give us directions?...OK, let me see if I have gotten it right. We take Route 161 up to New Sweden and get off on Westmanland Road and go left. Westmanland swings around and goes north. We continue for about mile and a half and look for a dirt road that takes off to the right. The road is just to the south of Fogelin Hill. Your cabin is on Fogelin Pond. OK. We will tap on the horn when we get there. We are driving a rust colored Chevrolet. See you soon."

"Those directions are much like driving through a corn maze."

"With an expert navigator like you, how could we go wrong?"

"You can sum up everything I know about navigation in one word. Garmin."

Another attempt at levity that has fallen flat.

"If you get us lost up there even the Saint Bernards won't find us."

We do get there and find the driveway to Gustafson's home which is right on the pond. It's a log cabin affair at the very end of the driveway. We tap the horn as instructed. The door opens and out onto the porch strides Moose's uncle with a shot gun in his left hand aimed at the ground. He's a grizzled looking guy, tall and thin with a beard and bright shiny eyes underneath bushy eyebrows. I step out of the car, hold out my hand and am to greet him when two beefy dogs come tearing around both sides of the house. They screech to a stop on a sharp command from Gustafson.

"Don't pay any attention to them. They won't bother you. Just hold out your hand so they can get used to you and I'll let them roam."

I do. They do. The two of them of sniff around me for a few seconds and the promptly lose interest in me.

"Now the lady."

We go through the same routine with Silvia.

"Well don't just stand there. Come on up and make yourselves ta home."

We climb up the few steps to the porch level

and he holds out his hand which I grab and am surprised with a very strong grip. Hard to tell how old this guy is, maybe as old as I am, but it's clear that he has taken good care of himself. In my mind, I wonder how one gets to a hospital way out here or even just a Doctor's office without kicking the bucket first.

"Come on in. I have some coffee on the stove. Moose has told me all about you. I understand that some bad guys are after you. I hope that you have the means to protect yourself. You can't depend on the police in a situation like you're in."

"We've just come from Big Al's shooting range where we've been learning how to use the handguns he sold us. I thought it best to leave them in the car."

"If you hadn't, I might not have been able to keep the dogs off you. They are very protective of me."

I try to hide the shudder of my body.

"That offer of coffee sounds good to me," as I quickly change the subject.

The inside of the cabin is clean and comfortable looking. Sparsely furnished but the floors are covered with rugs that are probably from some animal or another. The place is pretty much one big room with a kitchen in one corner and a bed in the other corner at the rear. The area on the right hosts a large stone fireplace. This looks like a living/dining area. The furniture looks handmade. I expect by Gustafson.

"This is a great place. How long ago did you buy it?" I ask like a fool.

"I didn't. Built it by myself along with everything in it. Twenty-six years, ago."

"Does the fireplace heat the whole place? I noticed a large stack of firewood outside?"

"Nope. I have a propane heater for when it gets really, really, cold, which it does for nearly three months of the year. Can't get delivery way out here so I haul it here in small tanks. They are out back, along with my pickup truck under a small shelter up against the back wall. I'll show you later." He is proud of his handiwork.

"This coffee is great," Silvia speaks up. "I'm impressed with your kitchen. All those copper pots and pans look like they came out of some fancy kitchen in New York."

"Those were all my mother's. Brought them here when I first came."

"And I'm impressed with your immense library," I add.

"Some of them belonged to my parents but

most of them I bought myself over the years. Many of them I haven't read yet. I don't have television, nor do I want it, so I read a lot. In the summer, I tend to the wood pile, hunt some and fish some. In the winter, I cross country ski for fun. Hunt and ice fish for food."

"It sounds like a fairly lonely existence," pipes up Silvia. In other words, she is asking him about girlfriends.

"Not really. I have friends in town and neighbors out here. Occasionally someone will stop by for coffee or a game of chess. It's not as lonely as it may seem to you."

"As pleasant as this short visit has been, I have what could be an unpleasant question to ask you."

"I'm guessing that I already know what that is. You want to know if you can hide out here if the bad guys get too close. The answer to that is yes."

"It might not be as simple as that. These guys have help everywhere around the globe and assets we don't even begin to know about."

"Bring them on. It could be fun. I can't guarantee that I can protect you by myself but my friends around here will help and at least we'll give them a good fight. Don't forget we know this land and they don't."

"If you are positive about this, I will accept your offer. But I want you to think about this carefully for a few days. We are going back to PI. I'll call you when I know more about our situation. Many thanks for listening to us."

"My pleasure. Have a good drive back to PI."

Silvia drives on the way back to Caribou and then to PI.

"What's your take on Gustafson?" She asks.

"I think he would be a formidable opponent, particularly on his home ground. While we don't know his neighbors and friends I suspect that they would be similar types of characters: strong, self-sufficient, and people not to be trifled with. If I had to put my life in someone's hand, I don't think I could do much better than Gustafson and his friends."

"I agree with that. One thing we didn't discuss with him is another way out of his property. I have already checked out maps of this area, so I know there are other roads that will get us to the Canadian border and on to the St. Lawrence Seaway if we choose to go in that direction."

"We've talked about that before and that's a good alternative as far as I am concerned. Easy to sneak across the border without any paper trail. And there are so many ways to go from there. North into Montreal, Quebec or some smaller town. Across to the great lakes and middle America. I think the Nazis would have a tough time finding us up there. The key of course would be to make sure we don't get trapped in New Sweden."

"For now, we had better get back to PI and keep our eyes and ears focused on what's happening in the area. We don't have any reason to believe they are in the area at this point."

Too late to do any work back at the paper so we go on to the apartment. I do telephone the paper to see if there is any breaking news. Everything is quiet there. We eat dinner, watch a movie and go to bed. Just like a normal couple. The nights are getting cool up here even though it's only September. I hope we are home before the snow starts, but only if the Nazis are in custody or dead. I prefer dead. I sleep poorly, get up several times to go into the office and crank up the Toshiba. I search the news channels without a clue what I'm looking for. I find nothing and am in such a fog that I wouldn't know if I *was* staring at a news item that was relevant to our plight. After about four hours of that nonsense, I am so tired that I am asleep before my head hits the proverbial pillow.

Silvia misses nothing as everyone knows, so when I sit down for breakfast she takes one look at me and asks, "Do you want me to take you to the hospital or shall we go directly to the morgue?"

"Have a little pity. After all it was your snoring that kept me awake."

"Right. Poor baby. It's as bad as I thought. You are just hallucinating. We will skip the hospital and the morgue and just find you a shrink who likes the most difficult cases."

"I'm finding your humor very crude and not at all funny this morning. What's your plan for the day?"

"I am a professor so I don't have to do anything. However, I am going off to my office at the University to plan my next lecture. Who knows, there may even be a struggling student or two who drop by for help. And you?"

"I suppose I will continue my defense of freedom of the press at the office. You can drop me off if you will dispense with any more of your sick humor. Otherwise, I will walk. Perhaps the fresh cool air will clear my head and a good idea for another feature story will fill the void."

"I'll not touch that one but let me drop you

off. Fresh cool air can be overdone."

I sit for a while at the office and think about the possibilities for some new feature stories. Given the importance of the potato industry in the area, there may be a good story there. But only if I don't have to muck around in the fields myself. Ok. I'll put this on my list with priority. That leads me to question myself: what role does the potato play, in terms of the overall economics of the region and what's ahead in terms of future development? I know the area produces maple syrup but I don't know the scope of the product and whether there's a story lurking among the maple trees. I will check this one out because it may end up being a sweet story. Don't tell Silvia about this feeble attempt at humor. The history of UMPI is well known but maybe a story based on the faculty members would be of interest. I'll check this out with Silvia.

I stop by the office and seek out Steve. After a few minutes, he waves me into his office.

"What's up, Harry?"

"Well I've been searching for another feature and what I've come up with is a story on the importance of the potato to Aroostook County."

"Stop right there. We've been there and done that. In fact, more than once. Get out of the office and dream up something different."

I find Silvia at home and explain that Steve has vetoed my idea about the Potato Feature.

"I don't know what to do," say I. "My mind is just a blank."

"I don't think I will touch that one. But seriously let's take the afternoon off and just walk around town a bit."

"Ok. I don't suppose you'd like to like to clear your head with lunch at the Sorpreso?"

"No. I would not. I'll make you lunch right here. I can tell you are down, so I will also wash and dry the dishes. Put your mind in neutral for the rest of the day and just relax. Something will pop up. I know it."

"How about we go over to UMPI's Reed Gallery and see what uplifting stuff they are showing?"

"Ok. As long as we don't have to plow through stuff like Andy Warhol."

"As a matter of fact, the gallery has some original works of his. I'll pretend I'm blind and you lead me through it."

"It will be a pleasure to lead you anywhere. I hope all my colleagues at the 'U' are there to see who is boss in this family."

"The boss makes lunch while I catch up on all the news."

"That ought to cheer you up."

"I'm sure it will."

While she makes me a pastrami sandwich and some potato salad, I read the papers.

When I sit down at the table I say to her, "What I have learned in just a few minutest is the world continues to be in a state of turmoil. The Mideast situation continues to simmer and our president has not yet learned how to say Islamic Terrorist. Neither has Hillary Clinton, the Democratic candidate for president. On the Republican side, Donald Trump's hair shows no signs of improvement. Both candidates are too old to be president and we only hear second hand rumors about their health. We have had rough periods in our history before and have survived many difficult times. I hope we will again. I remind myself that our own personal survival is most important to us just now. I can't afford to get too depressed about national and international events. Easy to say, hard to pull off.

"Thanks for lunch dear lady. I think it's picked up my spirits a bit."

"You are the only person I know whose mood can be elevated by potato salad."

"Hey. The mere mention of the word potato reminds me of all the time I wasted in doing the research for a feature story on the evil vegetable."

After she does the dishes, we agree to go over to Reed's Gallery. It's a fine day, so we walk.

Even Andy Warhol doesn't spoil our 90 minute tour of the entire gallery. In one corner of the gallery we stumble onto an exhibit of children's art. I am stunned by some of the work and can't believe it's been done by grade school students.

"Silvia, maybe we have just stumbled onto a good feature story. I'm going to find out what school these kids are from and then pick out the most promising work. Look, this still life of some flowers on a table is terrific. It's an oil and was painted by a seven-year-old girl. I'm going to take down her name and go over to the school to talk to her and her teachers."

"Not now you aren't. We are on our way home. I've got a surprise for you."

"Really. What is it?"

"Won't be a surprise if I tell you now. Would it?"

"I guess not."

"Besides it must be seen to be enjoyed."

"I love surprises and I suppose that it wouldn't be a surprise if you told me. Do we walk to it?"

"No. We go home and get the car and drive to it."

"I was envisioning a surprise right here at home."

"Maybe later."

Off we go on Route 1, toward the south.

"Oh goody, we are going to Key West. A splendid surprise."

"Almost, but not quite."

We drive the few miles to the entrance to Aroostook State Park and turn in.

"Here we are. One-thousand acres of wooded trails."

"This is it? One-thousand acres of what?"

"Beautiful scenery, fresh air and solitude. Don't be a grump. Follow me."

We end up walking for several hours, enjoying the solitude of the park, walking, watching the wild life, laughing and totally relaxed. We forget the country's troubles and most importantly our own troubles.

"I'm a convert," say I. "Can we just stay here for a week or so?"

"Nah, I forgot to bring a tent, and enough of your favorite ice cream."

"Maybe we just sleep out under stars."

"You mean with the wolves, bears and

snakes?"

"Um, let's go home."

"That's what I thought, oh brave warrior."

We drive straight home and crawl into bed. Does anyone really "Crawl" into bed?

"I think a movie would interrupt my mood. I am refreshed and full of energy."

"I think so too. Anything else you can think of to do?"

"Um, yeah, it's about that blunt instrument you talked about earlier today."

"That's funny. Maybe I made it up."

Much later we are sound asleep for the rest of the shortened night.

In the morning, I drive to the school where our girl-wonder goes and talk to her art teacher. She tells me that Ann, her student, has been painting since she was five years old. I can't believe it but her teacher drags out a large portfolio of her work and I become a believer.

"May I talk to her? I'd like to do an interview with her for the paper and include some of her work. Would that be possible?"

"Well, I can't speak for her parents but I bet that they would be delighted."

"Great. Let me check it out with my editor and I will get back to you. I know he will want to do the story and it will just be a matter of picking out a time when we can get Ann and parents together so we can talk. I'll want to borrow some of her work for the story, as well."

"That's terrific, I look forward to hearing from you and in the meantime, I will call her parents and make sure it is alright with them."

"Super. You take care."

You too.

On the way home, I stop by the shop and sit down with Steve.

"I have an idea for a good human interest story and I want to run it by you before I do anymore work on it. I bumped into the art work of a young girl a few days ago at Reeds Gallery at UMPI and it was quite incredible. I spoke to her teacher today and she thinks her parents would be delighted to have us do a feature on her and include some of her work. How do you react to this?"

"Well, it sure beats potatoes. Sorry for that dig."

"If that's a pun keep working on your comedy line."

"Sorry, I couldn't resist it. Seriously I love the idea. Talk to her parents and see if they go along. Oh and by the way drag the teacher into the story. It will good publicity for her and the school."

When I get home, I see that Silvia is working away on some lecture notes in our office, so I stay away from our office.

"Hey," she hollers out. "What happened with Frederick?"

"He bought my idea to do a feature on the young artist. I am going to put that off for a day or two because it is time to tear that typewriter apart and see what I can find that makes it so sought after. I plan to start that in the morning and spend as much time as necessary. I am determined to figure it out. Would you mind if I set up a card table in the office and work there?"

"No. Not all. If you are going to be here, the revered professor will go to the U and work there."

"Ok, but I may need some help with this and you are the smartest person I know."

"Aw, how sweet. Just call if you need me. Now just go make dinner."

"I think I asked for that."

I make some spaghetti and meatballs for myself and some plain spaghetti without tomato sauce or meatballs for Silvia. I put some olive oil on her spaghetti. I would have added some tofu but I didn't think that would mix too well.

"Just one bite and I already know that it's delicious. As a reward, I think I will let you do all of the cooking until we get home."

"Gee, thanks. If you do the dishes, that's fine with me."

"Nah, you do them too. I keep telling you there is a price to pay for the services of a revered professor. What's so hard to understand?"

I might really need her help with what I find on the typewriter, so I defer.

"And, you are still the social director of this household so go find us some social for this evening. Then tomorrow you can do all the hunting on that typewriter that you need to."

"I'd be delighted."

After dinner, we watch *Big Stone Gap* with Ashley Judd and Whoopi Goldberg. I like it even if it is a chick flick. Sleep comes easily. I make an omelet for me in the morning with blueberry jelly and cream cheese along with home fries. I make oatmeal for Silvia with raisins.

"Thanks for the breakfast, slave. Now get to work and find out what makes that stupid typewriter so valuable while the revered and lovable professor goes to the U to think, study, and just generally make the world a better place to live. When and if you need help with your work, give me a call. Now, wash and wipe the dishes."

She gives me a peck on the cheek.

"Sure. Thanks. You go off and figure out how to make the world a better place while I stay here try to find a way to keep us alive."

CHAPTER XIV -
THE PUZZLE IS SOLVED

When she is out the door and the dishes are done, I begin to work on the Million Dollar Typewriter. I set the machine on a table in the office and just stare at it for a few minutes. The first thought is that maybe the simplest approach is the answer. That would be the serial number. This is etched in the case in plain view. It is S-61512956-12. It's a very large machine. It is ordinary looking. Its appearance offers no hints to any inherent value it might have. There is little call for big clumsy typewriters like this. Were it not for its history it would fetch maybe $100 on the market. Probably less. Remember, I paid $250 for one in PI. I needed it because I thought it might help me keep the MDTW safer. No one tried to steal either typewriter and I wish I had my $250 back now.

Ordinarily I would look at the MDTW and not have a clue to its history or potential value. An explanation how I found out about its history is in order. I received a telephone call some years ago, from a lady who lived in northern Massachusetts. She, or more likely her son, apparently got my name from an internet search. She told me on the phone that she wanted to bring the machine to my shop and have it restored. She made an appointment and a few days later she showed up with her husband and the Underwood.

She explained to me that her son found the typewriter in the trash at Columbia University where he was a student. He brought it to their home and hence to me

Now I am not the most knowledgeable person about history but I knew it when I saw it plainly spelled out for me. This typewriter has a tag affixed to the side that says it is the property of the U.S. Navy at the Physics Department of Columbia. I had read about the work of that department in the past. Just before WWII, Enrico Fermi escaped Italy with his Jewish wife and came to the USA. He and our War Department knew that the Germans were working on a nuclear device. Fermi enlisted Albert Einstein to sign a letter to President Roosevelt asking for funds to set up a lab and continue his research. The part of this story that had led me to read about it was the fact that Einstein's only help on this project was to sign the letter to Roosevelt that Fermi drafted. Einstein was a pacifist and retired to the safety of Princeton University and offered not one stitch of help during the war, to the country that gave him refuge. I didn't understand it when I read it then and I still don't. We won the war, at least in part, because Fermi beat the Germans to the atomic bomb while Einstein sat on his butt at Princeton. I still get angry about that even today.

If I could prove that the letter to Roosevelt was typed on this machine it would no doubt be worth tens of millions of dollars. One way to do this would be to get a sample of typing from the typewriter and compare it with the typing from the letter. I explained all this to the woman (I don't remember her name). I told her that it would be unwise to restore the machine because it might ruin all chances of comparing its typing to that of the letter. The best thing to do, I explained would be to remove the ancient ribbon and replace it with a new one and get a sample of the output to compare with that of the letter. That would require obtaining a copy of the letter for the comparison. She said she would get a copy and send it to me. I gave her $20 to cover her expenses in coming up here. She did send me a very poor copy of the letter but I never heard from her again. Obviously, I have the typewriter but not any proof that I own it. I obtained a good copy of the letter from the National Archives. There was no obvious way to link the typewriter with the letter. I do know that the machine was in Fermi's lab by 1942 and that important documents were undoubtedly typed on it.

Since the machine was manufactured in 1914, I drop the serial number as being at all related to the machine's hidden secrets or its value. If this is the case, then there is something in the machine itself that will solve the puzzle. I sit and study the machine for a few minutes. I see only one obvious way that anything could be hidden in it. That would be under the keys. I carefully begin to remove the nickel rings and the paper inserts underneath under each one. I start with the middle row (Letter Q) and I find nothing at all. I drop down (Letter A) and repeat the process. Nothing. Perhaps there is nothing to find under the keys. I start to doubt that I will find anything thing at all. I am stubborn, if not very smart, so I continue with the row beginning with the letter Z. Nothing. Now I really begin to doubt my assumption that the clues are under the keys. Only one row left and that is the top one, which begins with the number 1. PAYDIRT!

There are letters under the numbers. I had avoided looking here at first because I thought that it was more likely that the clues, if they were here at all, would be under the letters. I mistakenly assumed that there might be a relationship between the letter on the outside and the one underneath.

What I find are the following letters of the alphabet.

BAPPAZHANS

They do not spell out any words that I know about. Nor do I see any clue as to what they do mean. I need a better brain than my own to figure this out and there is only one professor of English in the family. Silvia's at the University and I decide not to interrupt her, much as I want to do just that. I make a simple lunch which consists of a roast beef sandwich and some potato salad. I really didn't need the potato salad but I consider it a vote of confidence in the region's most important crop. I hide the MDTW under some dirty clothes in the closet, along with the parts I have removed. The inserts with the letters on them go into the pocket of my running shorts. Running will make the time go faster. If I time it right I should be back before Silvia gets here. I guess wrong on that one. When I get back the car is parked at the apartment.

"There you are! I called and when you didn't answer, I got frightened and came right back. I see by your attire that you were doing what you call jogging."

"Sorry. I didn't have my cell with me. And I forgot to take the apartment key with me. Good you are here."

"Sounds to me like you are in your usual befuddled state of mind."

"Not kind, woman. You should be impressed with my detective skills for I have uncovered a clue to what makes the MDTW so valuable."

"Don't keep me in suspense any longer. What is it that makes it worth more than $250?"

"Hey. I said I found the clue but I didn't say I knew what it meant. For that we need the sharp mind of a university professor."

"If you need someone with the highest credentials I will volunteer. But only after I've had some lunch. Judging by the dirty dishes in the kitchen you have already eaten. Forget to do them?"

"I was too excited to worry about a detail like that."

"Show me what you found and I will study it while you make me lunch and do the dishes."

"I wish you'd get off that kick." I see the raised eyebrow. *"OK, OK."*

I show her the letters I found which I have written down in the proper sequence. I also show her the actual inserts, again in the original sequence. I leave her alone while I make her a large garden salad. When I have finished, I bring it into the office and plunk it down on the table.

"How's it going?"

"Give me some time. And don't stand over me. Wait somewhere else."

As I walk away, I notice that she is opening the Toshiba. I hope that means she is making progress. A while later she beckons me to appear.

"I know you're standing just outside the door so come on in now. Sit down over there and you can do the dishes later."

All this with a smile on her face that tells me she has made some sense out of this jumble of letters.

"Pull up a chair and follow me through my reasoning. If anything does not make sense, let me hear your thoughts. First, the last four letters HANS is clearly a Germanic name."

"I agree."

"Um, just let me know when you disagree. OK?"

"Sorry."

"OK. Where did most of the Nazis fleeing Germany at the end of WWII go? They went to Argentina. What is the largest city in Argentina? Buenos Aires. So, I'm thinking the first two letters BA stand for that city. Are you with me?"

"I am."

"It makes sense to me that the fleeing Nazis brought with them a vast amount of treasure. It couldn't be cash because the German currency was worthless at that point. It's not logical they could have laid their hands on any significant amount of gold bullion or precious jewels. Maybe, but I lean toward discarding it as unrealistic for the moment. We do know that Nazis plundered a large collection of artworks. The other letters, PPAZ, I have drawn a blank on. Any ideas?"

"Please excuse me, if I do some thinking out loud. If we accept your idea that the Nazis took artwork to Buenos Aires, how would they likely keep or display it? If it were in a public museum it would be subject to scrutiny by the entire world. They don't want that. It would be dangerous to hide them away in a storage facility. Besides they would never get the pleasure of looking at them. Therefore, it follows that the treasures are more likely housed in a place owned by a person or group of persons where they can be displayed. If they wanted to, they could invite selected persons in for a private showing. Even try to sell them if they need the money. This suggests to me the conclusion that the letters PPAZ represents a large private building in or near Buenos Aires. A large building where a person or persons live. I am drawing a blank where we go from there. The ball is back in your court."

"I follow your line of thought. Toshiba to the rescue. Let me do a google search."

She runs a search on art museums in or around Buenos Aires first. All the museums we find can be accessed by the public. Logically, we rule them out.

"Try a search on large warehouses."

"OK."

That search produces a selection of industrial buildings that would seem unlikely as places to exhibit valuable works of art. It doesn't make sense to us that anyone in their right mind would store art in a building on the waterfront beside a railroad track. Maybe that would seem so unlikely that it would be a brilliant idea.

"Put that one aside for the moment and we will come back to it if nothing else more promising turns up. Try a search on mansions in the area and see what comes up."

"Oh, there are quite a large list of mansions there."

As she scans the list, I see her eyebrows raise, followed by a sharp intake of breath.

"What?"

"I believe our search is over. Look at this one, Palacio Paz. Call the FBI, the State Department, the United Nations, who knows. Pack our bags and let's go home."

"Whoa. Not so fast. All we think we know is where some art works are in Buenos Aires. We can't prove anything and it is not likely that the FBI will do anything but maybe attract some attention our way. I can see it now, 'Looney Couple in Northern Maine Claim to Know Where WWII Treasure Is. Couple living with False ID Papers'. I don't think we want that to happen. Too risky."

"Well what do we do?"

"Nothing yet. We should go on about our normal business for the next few days. That will give us some time to develop a rational plan that will get us out of this predicament."

"Lord, I don't know if I can do that."

"Sure, you can. We've been up here this long, what's another few days?"

"Oh alright. But if you see flames coming out of my mouth and steam out of my ears be kind and gentle with me."

"I promise."

"Do you have any semblance of a plan lurking in the back of your brain?"

"No. None, at all. That's why I need some time."

"Hey dude, it's three o'clock and we haven't even had lunch yet. Hold on a minute and I'll see what the Toshiba says about the subject of pizza. Should be a piece of cake for it after all the hoops we've had it jump through today. Ha. Grab your keys, carry me to the car and let's go to Rosella's. It's a bit father then some of the other places but Toshiba gives it a 4.1 rating out of a possible 5."

"Suits me. Let me go to the potty and throw some cold water on my face and I'll be ready."

It's just a short drive to Rosella's and when we get there we decide to eat there rather than take it back to the apartment. It's long after lunch time and well before dinner so the place is quiet and thinly populated.

Our pizza is ready in 20 minutes. It arrives piping hot. (What in the world is piping hot?).

"I must tell the Toshiba that its advice was perfect. English professor, where does piping hot come from?"

"Near as I can remember, it dates to medieval times and refers to the steam that shot out of a spouted tea kettle. Such a device was in use in ancient Mesopotamia."

"My goodness. The word-queen really knows her stuff."

"A piece of cake for me. You haven't forgotten that I am a revered professor of English, have you?"

"How could I forget when you remind every hour on the hour like a cuckoo clock?"

"This pizza is wonderful," says she, deftly changing the subject.

"Yes, it is. Remind me to pat Toshiba on the back when we get home. It's not the Café Sorpreso but it did the job."

We finish our meal, compliment the chef, pay our bill and head back to the apartment.

"Revered Professor, I think I have another treat in store for you," I say when we get home. "Several staff members at the paper recommended a movie to me called The Confirmation. Let's go to the big screen and watch it in the bedroom."

The movie co-stars Clive Owen and Jaeden Lieberher. Owen is the farther who has an alcohol problem. Lieberher is his 8-year old son. The boy's mother has divorced his farther who struggles and overcomes the alcohol problem with the help from his son and some from his mom.

"That was a touching story and a good choice, Harry. Thank your friends at the paper for me. The kid was sensational, a natural born actor if I ever saw one. Spoke with looks, his mouth, his eyes and his body. Good job and good night."

"Is that all. No rewards for serving as social director and solving our riddle?"

"That's correct. And you haven't solved the riddle yet. Good start though. Keep up the good work and good night."

With that and a peck on the lips she is off to sleep in seconds. My mind is in a turmoil as I lay awake. I can't shut off the constant roller coaster search for a way out of this quagmire. One dead-end after another. Hours later I quietly climb out of bed and tiptoe to the office. I decide to invest some time in planning Ann's story for the *Herald*.

"Good morning, loveman. I tried not to wake

you. I take it you were up late? Duty calls and I am off to my post at the U."

"Really. What time is it?"

"Almost ten."

"Crap. I've got to get to the paper before I'm fired."

"Don't you remember? The boss gave you some time off."

"Oh yeah. I should kick myself in the behind for staying up so late to work on a feature story. Don't do that. I'll do it for you when I get home. Bye now. I'm out of here."

Left by myself, I fall back asleep and don't wake up until 2 o'clock. Its way past breakfast time, too late for lunch and too early for dinner, so I make myself a combination meal. Pancakes with maple syrup and a steak with sautéed onions. I am so stuffed that I probably won't eat again today. I need some physical exercise so I put on some little boy pants (shorts to those of you are not up to date on the latest language innovations) and running shoes. I spend several hours jogging to and around Centennial Park. This is the most exercise I've had in a long time. It shows. By the time, I get back home I'm out of gas and ready to do nothing. Nothing at all. Before I've got the door closed, Silvia is on the attack.

"You could have left me a note or called me on the cell to let me know you were going out. I was very worried."

"You were?"

"Wouldn't you have been?"

"Yes. I would. Sorry."

"Apology accepted. I'm going to cook dinner."

"I'm not too hungry. I'll just have a salad."

I really don't want a salad but I figure it may gain me a few points with her.

"Wonders never cease. I'll make dinner so you can check out movies for tonight. Or we can watch the Red Sox."

"Or we can do both."

As I am munching on my salad, Silvia asks me if I have done my work as social director for the night.

"Indeed, I have. I recommend one of two movies. The first one is *Room* and the second one is *Amelie*. I don't know very much about either one, but we can explore and choose one. And then we will have time to watch all or part of the Red Sox game."

"Deal. Do the dishes and I will get into something more comfortable."

Something more comfortable turns out to be her PJ's. Nothing too exciting there. The Sox win another and appear headed for the World

Series. But they appear headed that way every year to devout Sox fans. Who knows? Maybe they win the series and the Patriots take the Super Bowl. The Celtics appear to need a big center or a "go to" guy and I can't watch hockey on the TV. Or in real life either. Just no interest. I don't remember much about the movie so maybe I slept through it. That's been known to happen. We both get a solid eight hours of sleep.

Silvia drops me off at the paper at 8 am and heads for the "U".

When I get into the press room, Frederick spots me and says, "Hey I thought you were going to take a couple of days off?"

"Days off are like retirement; vastly overrated."

"I know lots of retired folks who are having the time of their lives."

"They're well off, yes?"

"Most of them are comfortable. Have money to travel. Some take up hobbies that they never had time for before."

"Well I still think retirement is overrated for most people. I am going home to think about some new ideas for major feature stories to cover the gap left by your deep sixing my potato extravaganza."

I get out the cell phone and call Silvia.

"Are you busy? I don't want to interrupt whatever you are doing."

"No problem. I'm just grading some papers. Are you ready to be picked up?"

"That I am. Whenever it is convenient for you."

"See you in 10 to 15."

When she does pick me up I talk to her in the car on the way home.

"Hey, kiddo. I need some ideas about stories that I might write to fill the potato gap. Any ideas?"

"Um, yeah. I might. I bought some maple syrup when I stocked up on food. Let me go get it because I remember it came from a local farm. Here it is. The Maple Moose in Easton Maine."

"Would you like to come along if I can arrange a tour for tomorrow?"

"Sounds like a nice change of pace. Maybe we can get a gallon or two as a sample. Make the story more realistic."

"Really? How so?"

"Give me a few minutes and I'll figure out a plausible rationale."

"Is this the woman who doesn't eat sugar?"

"Got to have something to put on those

pancakes I'm planning to make for breakfast the next thirty days."

"Funny. I'll call Maple Moose right now."

I call and sweet talk them into a tour tomorrow, anytime during the day that I like. I'm beginning to like this job as a reporter. Everyone's so accommodating.

"It's all set for tomorrow. I like this job more and more each day. Maybe I'll consider a new job when we get back home."

"You think that the name of this place has anything to do with our Moose in Houlton?"

"I rather doubt it but we'll find out tomorrow."

"We watch a movie while we are eating dinner. It's entitled *Words and Pictures*, starring Clive Owen and Juliette Binoche. At the very end of the film during the credits we look at each other and express the very same thought; does it really have to end now?"

"As social director for this evening you have done a magnificent job, old girl. This might have been the best movie I have ever watched."

"I agree on both counts. It certainly has put me in a very romantic mood. How about you?"

"I don't need a movie to put me in a romantic mood. All I need is you."

"How sweet. Turn out the lights and let's go

to bed."

Yes ma'am.

I am awakened at seven the next morning by the sound of Silvia clanging pots, pans and dishes around in the kitchen. I stumble out of bed and into the kitchen, half asleep and barely able to find my way.

"What in the world is going on? Why are you cooking in the middle of the night?"

"Go take a shower and open your eyes. It's seven thirty. Since you are unable to detect what I'm doing, I'll tell you. I am making the first meal of the day which is called breakfast. You remember what that is don't you?"

"Very funny. It's your fault that I'm so groggy. You kept me up half the night with that movie and you know what."

"Get in the shower, wimp. The pancakes and maple syrup will be ready by the time you are finished."

"Ok. I want bacon with my pancakes... please."

"I couldn't function in the morning without a hot shower. It wakes me up; starts the blood flowing and gets me moving."

"First, a bang-up job as social director. Next, a bang-up job keeping me up, and now a bang-up job as chef."

"I won't touch that. Eat up so we won't be late for the Kings at Maple Moose."

"Good, I'll write that one up when we get back and then go to our young artist feature. That will keep me busy for a while."

We are out and on the road by nine and heading toward Easton. I put the MDTW in the back seat and cover it with a jacket that I won't need.

"I wonder if there is any connection to the fact that the town is located near the eastern border of the state and its name Easton?"

"You're so sharp this morning. I married a genius. Comforting, indeed. Did you bring the directions?"

"Umm no. I guess I left them home on the piano."

"That line might have worked in grammar school but not now. Lucky I have their telephone number. Look for a gas station where we can fill up and I'll call from their pay phone while you do the gas."

I find a station in a few minutes and fill up the tank while Silvia goes inside and calls the Kings.

"We are not too far. I have the directions and will guide you there. They had out-of-town newspapers there and I bought a few."

She tosses the papers into the back seat and we are off. Once we arrive, we are greeted by the Kings. They are a stout appearing couple who are clearly proud of their farm.

"Come on and we'll show you around the place. You know, of course, that maple syrup season is months away but we have work to do on this place all year. Take care of the equipment and get it in shape, manage the grounds and plan out as best we can next season's production."

"How can you do that?" I ask

"We are always growing maple trees. This time of the year, we try to identify which ones will be ready to produce. We must balance that against the market trends so we don't over produce or under produce. We still consider this a part time job even though we have about 1,000 trees and produce about 500 gallons per year. We use a vacuum collection system and that involves 10 miles of tubing."

I had no idea producing maple syrup could be so involved.

"Impressive," I exclaim. "It reminds me of a small factory, way out in the open."

"It is just like that and seems to get more involved as we grow the business into what we hope will be a full-time endeavor for us."

We walk around the farm for an hour while they show us everything. I take a few pictures even though pictures of trees won't be very exciting. I make sure I have one of the Kings examining some of the collection system.

"I'm going to prepare a draft of the article and let you review it before it's published. I'd like to have your comments, so don't be bashful."

"We won't and we will be looking forward to seeing it. Thanks so much for coming out here. I hope you will come back next year when we are fully operational to see how all this stuff works."

"We would be delighted. Thanks for letting us look around the place. Bye now."

"Bye."

As we leave I suggest a diversion to Silvia.

"I think we need some more shooting practice, so why don't we drive up to Big Al's and get in some time?"

"Why not? I could use a different environment for a few hours."

"Guns and shooting are certainly different. Are you getting to like them?"

"Maybe a little. One day I may have to protect myself from a jealous husband."

"Really?"

"Just kidding dope. I love you dearly and always will. "

"We head back to Presque Isle and then north toward AL's place without stopping at the apartment."

We are greeted by AL inside the shop where he is waiting on a customer.

"Be with you folks in just a few minutes."

"How you doing? Just take your time, we are not in a rush."

He finishes up with the customer in another 10 minutes. He makes a sale, deposits a check in the cash register and wishes his customer well and turns to us.

"How are my newest sharp shooters?"

"We're good Al. We wanted to get in a few hours of practice. Ok?"

"There's nobody out on the range and I don't expect anyone. Go ahead, load up with ammo and go shoot as much as you want. Is anything wrong? Have the bad guys made any progress in finding you?"

"Not as far as we know. We just finished up an assignment for a feature story on a major maple syrup producer over in Easton. Neither of us wanted to go back to our offices on such a lovely day. So here we are. We'll try to sharpen up a bit and then maybe take a short hike in the woods if there is enough daylight left."

"Hey, if there isn't enough light left for the hike this afternoon, you could stay overnight at my cabin out in the woods and do it in the morning before you go back."

"Really. Silvia?"

"Sounds like fun. I'm on board."

"Good. Come on outside and I will show you how to get there."

Outside he points out a narrow path that goes into the woods.

"It's out thataway about a mile or so. It's a log cabin and the only one there at the end of the path. Make yourselves at home. You'll find it stocked with beds and blanket and pantry with all kinds of canned goods. I think I left some eggs in the fridge. Unfortunately, there is no woman's underwear anywhere near the place."

"I see you have a powerline strung out that way. Does it go all the way to the cabin?"

"Yes. It does. You guys let me know when you are finished shooting."

"We will. For sure."

By the time we are finished, daylight is waning.

"I'm glad we aren't going to drive back to PI

tonight. A night in a log cabin off in the woods sounds very romantic to me."

"It does to this wimp as well. Let's pay Al for the shooting and get over to the cabin before it gets dark."

After I'd paid our bill, I thank Al and ask him if I can't pay him for the use of the cabin.

"After all, if we couldn't stay here we'd be looking for a motel."

"Not a chance. Get out there to the cabin and have a relaxing and refreshing night in the Aroostook wilderness".

"Complete with electricity. Thanks, and see you in the morning. Oh, by the way, could I pull the car around back of the shop so no one can see it and be tempted to steal it?"

"No problem. Leave me the keys and rest assured it will be safe. I'll be here and up early so don't worry about waking me. Take care."

"Actually," I tell Sylvia, "I wasn't worried about the car but the MDTW in the back seat."

The trail out to the cabin turns out to be on a gentle incline most of the way.

"You know if it were not for the power line I might get lost out here. How are you doing? Ok?"

"I'm fine. Keep going."

As we approach it, the cabin presents itself

exactly as you might expect. Rustic probably describes it as well as any word. The door is unlocked and the interior is one large room with a kitchen in the far-left corner, a sleeping area (just a bed) in the far right and a living/dining area across the front.

"Look at that huge stone fireplace. I wish it were colder so we could start a fire."

"Somehow, I think you wouldn't like being in this place if it were cold, sweet wonderful woman."

"Right. Climbing that trail in the snow probably wouldn't be a lot of fun, either."

After checking out the fridge and the canned goods on several shelves, we decide on a meal of canned clam chowder followed by baked beans and hot dogs. No TV here, so after we eat we sit outside on the porch and listen to the quiet sounds of the forest. Quiet that is until there's a loud thrashing around in the brush off to our left.

"What the hell is that?"

"Silvia. I think that might just be a bear. What do you say we get our butts inside?"

"I saw a bear once in a zoo, so I'd rather not see one here," she says as we quickly go inside and close the door. "Do you think he could break down the door?"

"Nah. Not a chance," say I in what I hope is a strong and certain voice. My conviction hides the reality that I am hardly knowledgeable about bears. It works. I can feel Silvia stop trembling as we cuddle in bed. We've had a long busy day so we drop quickly off to sleep. We sleep until seven the next morning. That is to say, I sleep to seven. I am awakened by the smell of coffee and follow my nose to the source. Silvia is in the kitchen corner fixing breakfast.

"Good morning, sleepyhead. I thought I was going to have to shake you awake. I see your stomach got the best of you. Go wash up and we'll eat."

"You know we've been out of touch with the world now for what seems like ages. I'm going to get back on board if that radio over there works."

It does work and we get a few minutes of music before the station switches to the morning news.

"Good morning folks. It seven A.M. on a bright sunny day here in Presque Isle, Maine. Temperatures in the mid-seventies today with no chance of rain to spoil your day. We will get back to music in 5 minutes but first a short roundup of the news around New England. On the weather front we continue to suffer from a

severe drought with many local cities and towns instituting controls over unnecessary use of water for such things as watering the lawn. On the crime scene, we have news of some arrests for drunk driving and possession charges in the region. From down south in our neighboring state of New Hampshire we have a breaking story of a vicious murder in Exeter, New Hampshire. Details are sketchy at this hour but apparently, the victim was the operator of a printing shop. Police officials aren't releasing much information at this point. Neighbors, however say that the man was tortured before he was murdered. They say that there was blood everywhere. The District Attorney says the cops also found a hidden room where the printer supposedly prepared false documents. Police are thought to believe that he was murdered by a disgruntled customer or someone who he was partnering with in other criminal activities. Stay tuned for more details."

"Silvia. Oh, my God. They must be talking about Joe Fletcher!"

"And that probably means it was the Nazis who were responsible and they probably know our assumed names."

"And not very long before they find our address in Presque Isle."

"I'm really scared now. Time to call the police," she says as she gets her cellphone out of here fanny pack.

"No, no. Wait. Let's think this through. As clever as these bastards are and with all their resources, they may be able to track our cells. Don't turn it on. We need to call the FBI in Boston or Washington but we can't use our own phones. Let's use Al's landline for protection."

"Good idea. God. I can't stop shaking."

I put my arms around her and pull her close.

"Hang on. We'll be OK once we talk to them."

I wished that I believed that myself. We quickly do the dishes and straighten out the cabin and trek back downhill to AL's store.

We catch Al just as he is opening the shop. Fortunately, there is no one in the shop.

"Hi Al. How are you today?"

"I'm fine. You guys are up early. Is everything alright?"

"No, it isn't. We have a serious problem and I don't want to get you involved in it."

"Hey. Let me be the judge of that. Tell me what's going on."

"Al. The bad guys who we have been running from are really, really bad and they have unlimited resources. They are modern day Nazis from Argentina who have a humongous cache of artwork plundered from Germany at the end of WWII. We have recently discovered where it is and that is why they are trying to find us. We are a loose end they need to get rid of. I'd like to call The FBI for protection. I must assume they will be able to track us if we use our cell. So, I must find another phone."

"That's easy use my landline."

"Al, I don't want to risk disclosing your location and putting you in great danger. It's best that we just get out of here and look for some new cellphones and then call the Feds."

"Good luck finding a store that sells cellphones anywhere near here. Nope, use my landline and then I will round up a bunch of friends and neighbors. We will set up a perimeter around the place just in case your friends show up. Here. Call," says he as he leads me to his landline.

I take it and call information for the number of the Boston office of the FBI. After I've dialed the number and get the switchboard, I ask to speak to the Agent in Charge.

"Good morning. This is Maria. May I ask who is calling please?"

"My name is Harry Stein—I mean Murray Segal. This is a life and death emergency for me and my wife. I have information on the murder of Joe Fletcher in Exeter, New Hampshire, but I need protection as quick as I can get it."

"Hold on. I'm sure he will he will want to talk to you."

"Good morning, Mr. Segal. My name is Joe Johnson. I am the agent in charge of the Boston office. I know who you are and I'm glad you called. The murder of Joe Fletcher was an especially gruesome one. I'm glad you called in. I can tell you that there has been another development in the case."

"What's that?"

"A shady private investigator by the name of Herman Biggs has been taken into custody after trying to bribe a border guard at the Hamlin border crossing. He wanted the guard to let him know if a couple of U.S. citizens crossed into Canada. He was carrying photographs of you and your wife."

"Did he confess?"

"No. He has refused to say anything and would not even call a lawyer or anyone else. So, we don't know who hired him but he appears to fear them more than he does us or a long term in prison."

"Agent Johnson, my wife and I have been travelling under false ID information that was supplied by Fletcher. We were travelling with the false documents because we have some knowledge of a vast horde of plundered artworks that were smuggled out of Germany at the end of WWII. I could tell you the entire story, but I'd rather do that in person."

"OK. We wondered why you were running. Just sit tight for a few moments and I will call you back on a secure phone."

With that he hangs up. About 5 suspenseful minutes later the phone rings.

"Hi Murray. Now you can tell me where you are?"

"My wife and I are at a place called Al's Gun Shop in Caribou, Maine."

"Is anyone there with you?"

"Al, the owner is here. We have been learning how to shoot on his practice range. We are relatively safe here. He knows about our problem. He has promised that he and some of his friends will protect us. We feel relatively safe here. It is way out in the boondocks."

"OK. Here's what I want you to do. First, get rid of your cell phones. The Nazis may be able to track them and you can't take that chance. Leave them on and drop them in the back of a truck that is southbound. If they are able to track the phones, they will think you are coming back to Presque Isle. If they can't track them, no harm done.

"Second, stay where you are. On no account should you attempt to travel by yourself. Al should be able to protect you well enough. We have just checked on his background and he appears to be a solid citizen. I gather he is very familiar with the area. You are far safer with him then venturing out by yourself. We think that Biggs knows what kind of a vehicle you are driving and he may have let his clients know. Third, stay by the phone. We will call you back as soon as we work out a safe plan to get you out of there."

"One more question Agent Johnson and I'll let you get back to work. Have a husband and wife team by the name of Smith who supposedly live in Houlton, Maine shown up on your radar screen?"

"No, they have not."

"Thanks. We will sit tight and wait for your call. Wait, one, more question. Is it possible to put my 3 kids, Karen, Lisa and Paul under guard in case the bad guys attempt to use them to barter for our location?"

"We've already covered that and you can rest assured they are perfectly safe, as are their children. Are there any other loved ones we should worry about?"

"Just my sister Fran and her husband Mort. But they live in San Francisco and should be safe, since they are so far away. But to set my mind at ease could you put a watch on them, too?"

We spend a nervous hour waiting for Johnson to call back. When the phone rings I answer in a shaky voice.

"Hi, this is Johnson. Here's the plan. We are sending a small crew up to the Northern Aroostook Regional Airport. It's located in Frenchville. That's close to the Canadian Border."

"That's way up near Madawaska, isn't it?"

"Yes, it is. You drive up there now and our crew will meet you. We will either hide out with you there or fly you out to safety."

"Hold on Agent Johnson. We are not safe so long as these guys are free to roam. Let me suggest an alternative to your plan. We go to Frenchville but not to hide. You use us to lure the Nazis up there. In other words, you arrange some way for them to locate us. It can't be obvious or they will be suspicious."

"Are you absolutely sure you and your wife want to be used as bait for a group like this?"

Before I answer, I whisper the plan to Janice with a questioning look.

"You're in, I'm in. No questions."

"We're both onboard."

"Alright. This is the tricky part. I need some time to think it out. Call you right back."

Ten minutes later I get the call.

"Forget what I said about getting rid of your cell. Keep it turned off until you get to Frenchville. When you are with my field crew, turn it on and make one call to the Exeter Police Department. They will be expecting your call. Simply give them your name and let them know you have information about Fletcher's murder but you can't give it out over the phone. Tell them where you are and ask them to send a car up there to get you. If they are tracking your phone, that's all we need. If not, I feel sure they are watching the local P.D. and will follow any cruiser that leaves town. Any questions?"

"Nope."

Janice has heard only my half of the conversation so I bring her up to date on the FBI's plan. I can feel her do a slow intake of breath and begin to relax.

"It feels good to see the light at the end of the tunnel."

"It does. Let's get our stuff together and head on out until we are just a few steps from Canada and one step from freedom and home."

"Al, I'm sure you heard that the FBI is on the case. We are off to Frenchville to meet a field crew. Thank you for all you have done for us. I expect to write a feature story or maybe a whole series on our travels. Do you mind if I give you some plugs in it?"

"Absolutely not. Lots of people know about my shop and practice range, but not everybody. I may get some new business out of the publicity. But even if I don't, I'd like to thank you two for your patronage. More importantly for letting me help keep you safe. I will remember this for a long time. Now let's pack your car and get you on your way."

We pack our few belongings including the MDTW and are on our way a few minutes later. We both have mixed feelings as we head east on Route 89. Happy that the end of the ordeal is in sight but a bit sad to be leaving the places and people who hosted us through it.

"You know Janice, when this is all over I want to drive back home through Presque Isle so we can thank all the people who have helped us."

"That might take a while. But I'm for it."

We head east to pick up U.S. Route 1 which will take a few minutes more than the alternate Route 161 that goes directly north. I figure Route 1 will be a better road and more populated. It takes us about an hour and a quarter to reach the airfield in Frenchville. We are met there by the FBI crew. One of the agents named Erickson seems to be in charge as they hustle us into their jet.

"Mr. Segal. Good to see that you made it safely here."

"Thanks Agent Erickson. This is my wife Janice Wayne. No one is happier to be here than we are."

I am surprised that there are only four agents, including the two pilots on board so I ask, "The folks chasing us have huge resources and people and I frankly expected a larger group of agents. Do you have enough manpower here?"

"Relax. We are just the advance crew. We have flown up from Washington. The rest of the group is driving up from Boston and will be here within a few hours. Don't worry. You will be safe with us and we will able to match whatever the bad guys bring to bear. We'll bring the plane into the hanger and wait for the Boston crew to get here before you turn on your cell and call the Exeter PD. In the meantime, can I get you some coffee?"

"Sure, I'll have a cup."

"And I'll have some tea if you have it."

"Coming right up."

After they have moved the plane into the hangar we chitchat about meaningless everyday events. About an hour goes by before the Boston crew arrives in a caravan of three black SUVs. I count four agents in each car. I still wonder about being undermanned but I probably would feel the same if there were a hundred of them equipped with armored vehicles and tanks.

"OK, now turn on your cell and make the call to the Exeter PD."

We make the call which lasts only a few minutes. After speaking to the Chief, I hang up and look to Erickson.

"Do you have any idea when the Nazis will be here? How will we know when they are approaching?"

"Obviously, I can't know for sure. However, if they have all the resources you think they do, I expect they would fly here to Frenchville in their jet. Anticipating that, we have another car and a four-man crew outside near the taxiway. They will call us when the plane lands. We already have technical information from their flight plan on what we think is their plane. Our crew will take control of the plane to cut off any possibility of escape and depending on the number of guys that exit the plane, some of the agents will follow them and back us up. They are dressed in jump suits as though they were mechanics and technicians working on the airport."

"He had barely finished speaking when his cell beeped. "

"OK, we will be ready."
"The plane is approaching the landing strip. Everyone outside and take up your places behind the wind blocks out front."

The crew scrambles outside and when the door is open I can see that they have set up some barrier like devices. I guess they are supposed to block the exhaust blast from a jet plane. The overhead door comes down as Erickson turns to us.

"You will be safest here in the plane so don't move until I say so. We are in the very back section of the hangar. We have left two agents inside near the door, just in case the Nazis manage to breech it. That's highly unlikely. Just to make sure that the three of us are safe. You can see that I have an automatic weapon as a last resort. I'm sure that I won't need to use it."

He puts his cellphone to his ear and nods his

head up and down.

"They are here and have parked the plane out front. Six guys have left the plane and are cautiously approaching the door."

We hear a loud and commanding voice on a bullhorn.

"Put down your weapons. You are surrounded and can't escape."

And then the sound of gunfire.

"All clear, Agent Erickson," comes a voice over the bullhorn

"You guys stay here. This is a crime scene that I don't want polluted. I'll come get you in a short while."

When he leaves, I start to get out of the plane.

"Murray, are you nuts? That was the FBI that ordered you to stay here. What part of that didn't you understand?"

"Aw. I'm going to stay in the hangar. But you know I am a reporter and I just want to take a peek."

As I step down out of the plane, I am confronted by a scene from a horror movie. The pavement is littered with bodies. There is what seems like a river of blood. The FBI Agents have cordoned off the area and are busily processing the scene, taking photographs and measurements. When I go back into the plane, I notice a couple of bullet holes in the top of the hangar door. Whew.

"Don't go anywhere near the door, hon. It's a nightmare," I caution. "There are bodies everywhere and judging by the amount of blood on the pavement, none of the Nazis survived."

"Not a sight I want to see. I'd have nightmares forever."

It's 30 minutes before Erickson returns to the plane.

"My guys are working on the scene and will be here for hours. Now, the first thing I need from you two are separate statements about what happened here today. The second thing I need is to know everything about the plundered art treasures and how you learned about them. But since they are in a foreign country, I want to wait on that until a representative of the State Department gets here. She is on her way here now but won't be here for a few hours.

"I'll get you some pads of paper and pens so you can sit in the cabin and handwrite your statements. Don't compare notes with each other. We know what you each remember about these horrendous events will not be the same. Don't worry about that because they never are. More coffee and tea? There are some FBI special sandwiches back in that small fridge in the corner. Not the Stage Deli in New York but they are not bad. Help yourself."

We sit down and jot descriptions of today's events as best we can. We follow instructions and don't compare notes. It takes us 45 minutes before both of us are finished. We sit and rest our weary bones for another hour while the Agents continue to work the scene. Before too long I hear a siren outside and when I look I see some local police officers arrive. I also see an elderly gentleman in what looks like hospital scrubs. I judge him to be an undertaker or the coroner or both.

We are both starting to tire. I catch Erickson a bit later and ask him if we can go find a motel for the night.

"Look, we are going to be here all night and you are welcome to stay here. Not the Ritz but reasonably comfortable. That will give us time to talk to Rita Carlson, the State Department Rep. who will be here within the hour."

"Well OK, just so we will not be in your way."

"You certainly won't. There are some Kindles back there if you want to read."

Neither of us is very much interested in reading as you might well understand.

"Why don't I get the MDTW out of the car so

we can be ready for Carlson when she arrives?"

"No, I don't want you out there but if you give me the keys I will send one of the agents to get it."

"Here are the keys. There is a typewriter in the trunk. You might as well bring it in here."

They retrieve the MDTW a few minutes later and set it on a desk. Janice and I sit staring at it for a while.

"Who would have thought that our whole world would be turned upside down when that typewriter walked in the door?"

"Changed our lives but we will recover. I wonder whose lives will be turned inside out when the plundered art is recovered. How will the world know who the art belongs to? I can visualize a long drawn out process with no logical conclusion."

"Maybe. Maybe not. You never know, Jan, there might be some records discovered with the art that traces the sources."

"Maybe. But even if there is, there will still be a difficult, maybe impossible job of tracking the heirs to the original owners."

"That's true enough."

We drink more coffee and tea and just ponder what might happen to this treasure trove.

"I hope the art is not buried in some storage warehouse while the records are searched. Now that I think about it, one or more travelling exhibits would be a great solution. Let everyone in the world get an opportunity to see it. Why don't we present that idea to the State Department? Maybe our suggestion would carry some weight because after all where it not for us, the art might be buried forever in the mansion belonging to the Nazis. A terrible thought."

"I'm with you on that one. Make sure we don't forget to suggest that to her. In fact, let's start off the conversation with that suggestion and hope it does not get tied up in some bureaucratic mish mash."

"We are still a newspaper writer and a university professor. We could let the world know about our idea. Some light on the idea might apply some measure of pressure. We are not without resources and we let them know that. Yes?"

"Yes. I'm with you. We should prepare a lecture at the UMPI and a newspaper story on the subject when we stop on our way home."

"Much as I would prefer to go straight home, I think using our positions up here makes good sense. Let's work on that now instead of trying to find something to read on the Kindle."

It's ninety minutes before Carlson shows up. In that ninety minutes, we have helped each other produce a detailed outline for her lecture and the written text for a *Star Herald* feature story.

Erickson introduces us and we sit down around the desk to talk. She is smartly dressed and very official looking. Her demeanor is business-like.

"Nice to meet you two. I'm sorry that I am late but hopefully this won't take too long and you can be on your way home. First, I'd like to thank you in behalf of the State Department. You have put yourselves in great danger and done a great service to our country and the many people who will benefit from the recovered art treasures. I am sorry it took me so long to get here."

"Not a problem," I reply. "We made good use of the time to prepare a University lecture for Janice and a feature newspaper story for me on our run-in with the Nazis. We are going to stop in Presque Isle on the way home."

"First, can we go over how and what you have found out about the stolen art?"

"OK."

I lead her through the process by which I

obtained the MDTW and then how I discovered the clue to its location in Buenos Aries.

"I am aware of most of that information. We have a team on our way now to the Palacio Paz. Our team will notify the local authorities but only after the art is in our possession."

"What will you do with it after that?"

"We have not decided yet but we will undoubtedly take it out of the country and then put it in storage somewhere."

"That's what I thought. Let me suggest another idea concerning what to do with the art instead of sending it to a warehouse for who knows how long. Identifying the original owners and their heirs could take a very long time. All this while the art is hidden from the world. I would respectfully suggest that you think about our idea. Break up the artwork into several manageable travelling exhibits and give millions of people the opportunity to see them. I'm sure this would put the State Department in a good light."

"That is an interesting idea. I like it and will recommend it to the powers that be."

"If you don't need us for anything else we would like to start our trip home."

"Thank you so much for your help and cooperation. Have a safe journey home. I will try to let you know what happens from here on in."

We thank her and then find Erickson to thank him and let him know that we are on our way.

"I don't know about you Jan, but I am pooped and I want to stop overnight at the first decent looking motel we find."

"Lord, yes."

That turns out to be the Gateway Motel in nearby Madawaska. By the time we get there and find a bite to eat we are both as exhausted as we never had been before. Before we get in bed we call the kids to let them know we are safe. Then, we are sound asleep before we know it. Too tired to do anything more than hold onto each other. After breakfast in the morning we drive south on Route I. We make a small detour to the west and stop at Big Al's. We stay only long enough to briefly update him on the happenings at Frenchville and then drive to Presque Isle. The very next day Janice delivers her lecture at UMPI and I drop off the feature story at the *Star Herald*. It takes me an hour to make the rounds at the paper. After that it's back to UMPI, where I pick up Janice and we begin the trek to Exeter.

I keep wondering how and why the location

of the treasure ended up in the MDTW in the first place? Will we ever know?

Did the Nazis have a spy in Enrico Fermi's Office?

If so, why didn't he simply let his associates know directly instead of using the uncertain means of the Million Dollar Typewriter?

How will the search for the original owners of the art treasures be found? Will they ever be found?

What will become of Herman Biggs?

Does this group of Nazis have associates who will try to retaliate against us?

Will our ordeal ever be over?

THE END